The king le ... **realize the** ... **the night with?"**

"Of course I do. Her ...

"Her name is Rosa C...

Kulal's expression remained unchanged, for he did not care to admit that the brunette's surname was news to him. "Mmm. That's right. Corretti. She's Italian," he said, as if imparting some important nugget of information.

"No, she is not Italian," said Hazail. "She's Sicilian. And not only is she Sicilian, but she comes from one of the most powerful families on the island."

"So?"

"So her brothers are probably going to come after you. In fact, the whole damned family is probably going to come after you after you compromised her reputation by spending the night with her."

Kulal shrugged. "Then let them come," he said carelessly. "For I am afraid of no man!"

SICILY'S
CORRETTI
DYNASTY

The more powerful the family…the darker the secrets!

Introducing the Correttis—Sicily's most scandalous family!

Behind the closed doors of their opulent palazzo, ruthless desire and the lethal Coretti charm are alive and well.

We invites you to step over the threshold and enter the Correttis' dark and dazzling world…

The Empire

Young, rich and notoriously handsome, the Correttis' legendary exploits regularly feature in Sicily's tabloid pages!

The Scandal

But how long can their reputations withstand the glaring heat of the spotlight before their family's secrets are exposed?

The Legacy

Once nearly destroyed by the secrets cloaking their thirst for power, the new generation of Correttis are riding high again— and no disgrace or scandal will stand in their way…

Sicily's Corretti Dynasty

Eight volumes to collect—you won't want to miss out!

Sharon Kendrick

A WHISPER OF DISGRACE

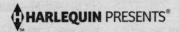

Recycling programs
for this product may
not exist in your area.

ISBN-13: 978-0-373-13176-1

A WHISPER OF DISGRACE

First North American Publication 2013

Printed in U.S.A.

HARLEQUIN®
www.Harlequin.com

All about the author...
Sharon Kendrick

SHARON KENDRICK started storytelling at the age of eleven and has never really stopped. She likes to write fast-paced, feel-good romances with heroes who are so sexy they'll make your toes curl!

Born in west London, she now lives in the beautiful city of Winchester—where she can see the cathedral from her window (but only if she stands on tiptoe). She has two children, Celia and Patrick, and her passions include music, books, cooking and eating—and drifting off into wonderful daydreams while she works out new plots!

Visit Sharon at www.sharonkendrick.com.

Other titles by Sharon Kendrick available in ebook:

To Tony "The Vet" Abbott…who is a fabulous person to see plays with and who has provided plenty of animated (geddit?) discussions and laughter over the years.

CHAPTER ONE

THE BOTTLE WAS cold, but not nearly as cold as the ice around her heart. Rosa lifted the champagne to her lips and drank another mouthful as she tried to dull the pain. She wanted to wake up and find that the past few days hadn't happened. She wanted to be the person she thought she'd always been. And she wanted that towering man on the other side of the nightclub to stop watching her with that dark and unsettling stare of his.

The flashing lights and loud music were making her feel giddy—or maybe that was just the champagne she'd been glugging from the moment she'd walked in. She wasn't really used to the sharp, bubbly flavour and she didn't really like it—mainly because she'd been brought up on the wines of Sicily which were rich and warm and red. Or at least, she'd been allowed the occasional half-glassful, topped up with water—watched over by the fiercely protective eyes of her two brothers.

Except that they were not really her brothers, were they? From now on, she had to start thinking of them as her half-brothers.

Rosa gripped the neck of the bottle, a shudder running down her spine as she forced herself to confront the unbelievable truth. That nothing was as it seemed, nor ever would be again. The discovery had been brutal and she'd found out in the worst possible way that she'd been living a lie all her life.

And she was nothing but a fake.

'*Mademoiselle?* You are ready?'

Wordlessly, Rosa nodded as the nightclub attendant gestured towards the podium on which various women had been attempting to pole dance all evening. It would be fair to say that most of them had been making an absolute hash of it, despite the fact that they were slim and blonde and incredibly fit. But then, all the women on this part of the French Riviera looked like that. Rosa was the one who stood out like a sore thumb with her mahogany hair, olive skin and the generous curves—which were currently spilling out of her brand-new crimson dress.

She placed one leg rather unsteadily on the podium, wondering if she would be able to dance in the kind of heels she wouldn't have dared wear back home in her native Sicily. But who cared if she stumbled? And who cared if her dress was the shortest thing she'd ever worn? Not her. Tonight she was going to shrug off the old Rosa, who had cared so much about appearances and doing the right thing. Tonight she was going to embrace a brand-new Rosa—one who had grown a tougher skin so that nobody could hurt her ever again. On this privileged strip of French coastline known as the Côte d'Azur, she would emerge from her protective shell into a glittering and unrecognisable creature—and her transformation would be complete.

She took another slug of champagne and put the bottle down, but as she stepped up onto the podium, she found her gaze locked with the man on the other side of the club—the one with the dark hair and the powerful body. He was still watching her—and something in the speculative amusement which glittered in the depths of his eyes made Rosa's stomach perform an odd kind of flip. Hadn't anyone ever taught him that it was rude to stare like that? And even more rude to ignore that poor woman who was practically draping herself over him.

The music began as Rosa gripped the pole, thrusting her pelvis towards it, the way she'd watched the others do. She'd never even seen a pole dance before tonight—nor would she ever have dared enter a competition for enthusiastic amateurs. But shock could make a person behave in a way which was completely out of character.

Snaking one leg around the slippery pole, she began to move. She could feel the smooth, cold metal sliding against her bare thigh. The alcohol was relaxing her and the hypnotic beat of the music began to suck her in. And suddenly it was easy. Easy to lose herself in the sensual sway of the music and forget about her own particular heartache. Her movements seemed instinctive—as if she had been born to dance this way. As if rubbing her body against a static piece of metal was the only way to go. Closing her eyes, she raised her leg even higher and tipped her head back, so that she could feel her long hair brushing against the floor. She began to grind her hips in slow and sensuous circles against the pole and, inexplicably, could feel the slow burning heat of excitement deep in her groin.

Through her dreamy reverie she could hear other sounds. A loud, whooping noise as she slid up and down in time to the music. The unrestrained clamour of male voices shouting enthusiastically as she clutched the pole and writhed against it. But Rosa didn't care who was shouting—she just kept her eyes tightly closed and gave the dance everything she'd got. It was the most cathartic thing she'd ever done and it wasn't until the music had stopped that she opened her eyes to find that a large crowd of men had gathered at the front of the stage to watch her.

For a moment she blinked at them, feeling like a prize exhibit being paraded in a foreign zoo. She found herself expecting to see the furious faces of her brothers.

Correction. Her half-brothers—but they were hundreds of miles away.

She straightened up and flicked her gaze over the assembled men, wondering how she was going to be able to make her way through them without pushing. Lots of them had their shirts open to the waist and their chests looked all sweaty. She didn't want to touch them. She shuddered. She didn't want anything to do with them. All she wanted was another drink, because the aching in her heart was starting to return and a drink seemed the only way to numb it. She bent to pick up the bottle, when she felt the whisper of fingertips on her arm and, straightening up, she found herself staring into the blackest pair of eyes she had ever seen.

It was the man from the opposite side of the club. The one who'd been staring at her. Who up until ten minutes ago had been the object of some beautiful woman's attention. She tried to focus her gaze to look at him properly, and as his image blurred and then sharpened again, she thought that she'd never seen a man like this before. Standing up close to his hard body and staring up into his hawk-nosed face, Rosa could suddenly understand why that woman had been draping herself all over him. He seemed larger than life—as if he was composed of some dark, elemental force which dominated the entire room. His black eyes glittered—as if a fire was smouldering behind those long lashes—and his lips were full and sensual.

But he frowned as he glanced at the clamouring throng of men. 'You look to me like someone in urgent need of rescuing,' he said, in an exotic accent she didn't recognise.

The old Rosa might have been intimidated by such a man—that's if she had ever been allowed to get within six feet of him by her overprotective family. But this new and tipsy Rosa was feeling no such thing as intimidation. Instead she looked into his eyes and felt an undeniable excitement—as if she had just found something she hadn't expected to find. Something she hadn't even realised she'd been looking for. 'And you're just the one to do it, I suppose?'

'I'm the perfect candidate for any kind of rescue mission, my beauty. Be assured of that.'

Trying to dampen down the excitement which was fizzing through her veins, she looked around her in mock surprise. 'But I can't see your white horse anywhere.'

'That's because I always ride a black stallion, although never in France. He's big and he's powerful and he's not particularly partial to nightclubs.' His eyes were gleaming as they gazed at her. 'Unlike a woman who doesn't seem to realise what havoc she was creating when she performed that incredibly sexy dance a few moments ago and nearly had the whole place in melt-down.'

Rosa's smile became a little glassy, aware that the level of flirtation was escalating by the second. And she was feeling more than a little daunted by it because this kind of thing was way outside her experience. Even during her university days in Palermo, the men she'd fancied had steered clear of her when they'd discovered who she was. Because what man in their right mind would get involved with a Corretti woman, a woman they wouldn't dare touch for fear that one of her brothers or cousins would come after them?

She'd never met anyone who hadn't been intimidated by the reputation of her powerful family and she wouldn't have been allowed anywhere near a man like this. A man who was sizzling out so much sex appeal that she wondered if her fingers might burn if she reached out and touched him.

She knew that the sensible thing to do would be to turn around and walk away. To go back to the hotel she'd booked into and sleep off the champagne. She would wake up in the morning—probably with a splitting headache—and decide what she was going to do with the rest of her life.

But Rosa wasn't feeling sensible. She was feeling... defiant. Because defiance was easier to deal with than heartbreak and loneliness, wasn't it? Defiance made you feel alive, instead of flat and empty and wondering just where your life was going. 'I don't want to be rescued,' she said, a touch petulantly as she took another swig of champagne. 'I want to dance.'

'Now that,' he said steadily as he removed the bottle from her hand and handed it to someone standing nearby, who accepted it without comment, 'can also be arranged.'

He took her hand and led her towards the dance floor and Rosa was aware of a sudden and heady sense of danger as he took her into his arms and the music began to throb out a sultry beat. He was so tall, she thought—taller than any other man she'd ever seen. And his body felt so strong. She licked her dry lips. A woman wouldn't stand a chance against a man like this. The thought thrilled her, rather than scared her as she knew it should have done. 'I don't even know your name,' she shouted.

'That's because I haven't told you.'

'And are you going to tell me?'

'I might—if you're very good.'

Recklessly, she said, 'And if I'm not?'

He didn't miss a beat. 'In that case, I will definitely tell you—because there is nothing I like better than a woman who isn't good. My name is Kulal.'

She tried saying it. Rounding her lips she sounded out the first syllable and then, letting her tongue touch the upper palate, she murmured the second. 'Ku-lal.'

'Mmm. I like the way you say it. It sounds very sexy on your lips.'

Rosa giggled. 'Stop it!'

With a sudden hard beat of lust, Kulal pulled her closer and felt her melt against him, as if she'd been waiting all night to have him do that. And wasn't it like that for him? Hadn't his senses been ignited from the moment he'd set eyes on her and seen those soft lips parting with a look of innocent wonder, which certainly didn't match the sinful splendour of her voluptuous body? He could feel the way her breasts were pushing against his chest and he sucked in a breath of longing as he dipped his mouth to her ear. 'Now let's see if you can dance as well on the floor as you did on the podium, shall we, my beauty?'

The slick words which flowed from his lips were warning Rosa to be careful. Because there was a reason for the expression 'paying' someone a compliment—her ruthless family had taught her that. You told a woman she was pretty and she would put out for you—wasn't that how it worked? Hadn't she grown up watching the male members of her family as they'd put their own heartless seduction campaigns into action? Men like this wanted only one thing from a woman like her and she'd been brought up to guard her honour and integrity. But that was before the world had changed. Before the values she'd held so dear had been held up as shallow and worthless.

So she pushed away her doubts and instead glanced up at him, batting him a coquettish look she hadn't even realised had been in her repertoire until now. 'You're going to mark me out of ten, are you?'

'If you want.' His hands tightened around her waist.

'But I warn you in advance that I can be a very harsh judge.'

The words came out almost before she realised she'd said them. 'I'll take the risk,' she said.

'Good.' His lips nuzzled against her neck. 'I like a woman who takes risks.'

Rosa could feel the whisper of his mouth on her bare neck and she closed her eyes with pleasure. This was... bliss. His arms had tightened around her and she realised that dancing with him was different to dancing with anyone else. He seemed to be making up the rules as he went along, completely ignoring the rhythm of the music and moving them around as if this was a slow waltz instead of a vaguely jumpy beat. And she was letting him. Why wouldn't she let him? Why, he could carry on doing that all night, he was so good at it.

'Do you like that?' he queried softly as the palms of his hands skated possessively over the curve of her bottom.

Her sudden, heady sense of freedom and the sensation of listening to her body's desires made Rosa bold and she didn't shrink away from the way he was pulling her even closer. 'Yes.'

'I thought so. I like it too. I like it very much.'

Kulal closed his eyes as he felt her fingertips move to his shoulders. He could feel the brush of her silken hair against his cheek and the wave of desire which swept over him was so strong that he was filled with an unbearable need to touch her more intimately.

But even though he'd always been known as a mould-breaking prince, Kulal respected his position enough not to throw his royal role into jeopardy. Dancing with a woman who was clearly an exhibitionist was one thing, but making love to her in a public place was quite another. So that even though they were shielded by the bobbing crowds around them and even though the flashing lights obscured most of their movements, he did not do what he wanted to do. Which was to play with the tips of her breasts through the thin satin of her mini-dress. Or to slide his hand up her thigh and touch the undoubtedly moist heat which would be searing its way through her panties.

That's if she was wearing any.

He swallowed, wondering if she could feel the sudden jerk of his erection.

He'd noticed her the moment she'd walked into the nightclub—but then, her shiny red dress had left little to the imagination. She had the type of body which was deeply unfashionable—especially here, in the South of France. She didn't look as if she spent hours at the gym and she didn't look as if she existed on a punishing diet either. The kind of diet which always left women with that furrowed and slightly anxious look—as if they were worried they might pass out from hunger. Instead she was ripe and luscious—like a juicy mulberry just before it fell from the tree.

He'd noticed the way her hair had tumbled like dark satin all the way down to her waist and her dress had skimmed the smooth expanse of her bare thighs. Their eyes had met across the dance floor—he had seen her eyes widen as if she had been surprised—and in that moment he had known. Just as he always knew when a woman wanted him. She was his for the taking and he wanted to take her as soon as possible—because one day very soon, this kind of sexual dalliance would be a thing of the past.

Kulal felt his mouth flatten in resignation, for the duty and the protocol of an arranged marriage loomed close on his horizon and his carefree playboy days were numbered. Even if he and his new bride were to agree to an 'open' marriage—or at least 'open' for him—he knew that in future he would have to conduct his affairs discreetly. He came from the kind of culture where wives turned a blind eye to their husbands' indiscretions, but marriage brought with it certain responsibilities. Gone would be the days of walking into a nightclub alone, and walking out with a beautiful woman on his arm.

He pressed his lips against the warm, fleshy shell of her ear as they moved in time to the music. 'What's your name?' he questioned.

'Rosa,' she replied, instinctively leaving off the 'Corretti' bit. He might have heard of her notorious family or he might not, but she wasn't going to take that risk. Tonight might be her night for behaving recklessly, but not stupidly.

'Rosa,' he repeated, running his palm down over the thick spill of her dark hair as if he was stroking the flank of his favourite mount. He smiled as he felt her wriggle in response. 'I like that too. Are you Italian?'

'Yes,' Rosa managed, even though it was difficult to speak when his earthy scent was overpowering her. Who cared that she was being a little economical with

the truth? She was Sicilian through and through, and
her family would have erupted with rage if they'd heard
her claiming to being Italian! But it was easier this way.
And she no longer owed her family anything, she reminded herself fiercely. Not a single thing. 'Yes, I am.'

'And do you make a habit of pole dancing in nightclubs, Rosa?'

She shook her head. 'Never done it before in my life.'

'Interesting. Why not?'

Rosa screwed up her face because this was a path
she didn't want to venture down. She shook her head.
'Tell me about you instead!'

But Kulal was coming to realise that he didn't want
to have to shout to make himself heard, and he didn't
dare stay on the dance floor with her much longer. Much
more of her rubbing her voluptuous body against him
and he would be unable to move. So why not cut to the
chase and continue this conversation somewhere more
private—like the seclusion of his villa complex, with
the convenience of a nearby bed?

'Why don't we go somewhere a little quieter?' he
suggested.

Rosa swayed. She wished he'd given her some kind of
warning before he'd loosened his grip on her like that,
because suddenly she felt like a ship which had broken
anchor. 'Like where?'

Kulal frowned as a flicker of irritation skittered over
him. Why did women always do this? Why did they pretend total innocence when they both knew exactly how
the night was going to end? Trying to suddenly play the
innocent was never going to work for someone as foxy

as her. He shrugged. 'I know a place with an amazing view, where we could sit and watch the stars.'

'Oh, I love the stars,' said Rosa dreamily.

'I love them too. So why don't we get out of here and find our own little piece of heaven?'

He made the words sound so poetic, Rosa thought as a feeling of wooziness shimmered over her again. She tried to remember the last time she'd eaten but it seemed like a long time ago. 'Okay,' she agreed carefully.

And Kulal smiled, for it was as easy as he had expected it to be. What Kulal wanted Kulal got. That's what they always said about him. He'd never had to fight for anything or anyone—except for the one person he'd really wanted, and it hadn't been possible to fight for her.

She was looking up at him now and the expression on her face was so soft and...trusting—and he didn't want her to look at him that way. He wanted her hard and hot and sexy. 'Let's go and find my car,' he said, his gaze skating over her bare arms and legs. 'Do you have a jacket, or something?'

Rosa blinked. Did she? She couldn't recall. She stared down at the satin minidress which was skimming her thighs. She remembered buying it in that ridiculously expensive boutique in Antibes just a few hours earlier, along with the towering shoes which complemented it. It matched the crimson bag which was hanging from her shoulder on a gilt chain, but she didn't remember it coming with a jacket.

'I don't think so,' she said vaguely.

The look that Kulal shot her was tinged with apprehension and, as he steered her through the packed dance floor, he suddenly began to regret his impetuous offer. She might look like every man's fantasy come to life, but now her gait was distinctly unsteady and he began to wonder just how drunk she was. He liked women who weren't good, that much was true, but he liked them to be sober.

His hand resting in the small of her back, he felt her stagger as they stepped outside the club and he caught her and steadied her. Thank God there were no paparazzi around, he thought grimly as he gently levered her into the back of the waiting limousine and she slumped back in the seat with her long legs splayed out in front of her, her eyelids fluttering to a close.

For the first time in his life, Kulal found himself tugging down the hem of a dress in a vain attempt to introduce a modicum of decency. Now was not the time to make the observation that she *was* wearing panties. Or that they were lace, by the look of them. 'Just how much have you had to drink?' he demanded.

That deeply accented voice penetrated her woolly thoughts and Rosa's eyes snapped open. The fresh air had made her feel very peculiar but suddenly she felt safe in this luxurious car. And he was still here, she thought. Her black-eyed rescuer from the nightclub who'd held her so closely on the dance floor. She felt very safe with him. So why wasn't he still holding her? Holding her so tightly that she could forget everything except the sensation of him touching her.

'Come over here and kiss me,' she mumbled as his jet-dark eyes swam in and out of focus, before the effort of keeping her eyelids open became too much and she closed them again. 'Please. Just kiss me.'

Kulal caught hold of her arms and gave her a little shake as he tried to wake her—but he didn't bother hiding his feeling of disdain, or his growing anger for having allowed himself to get into a situation like this. Did she really think that he wanted to kiss her when she was in that kind of state?

'Rosa,' he accused. 'You are drunk!'

'I know I am.' Her head lolled back against the soft leather seat as his unfamiliar words washed over her. 'And it feels fantastic.'

'If you could see yourself you would not think that,' he raged. 'For a drunken woman is never a pretty sight.'

'But a drunken man is okay, I suppose?' she mumbled. Because wasn't this what she'd grown up with? One rule for men and a different one for women. Oh, why was the world so unfair?

'I don't approve of anyone losing control of themselves in such a way as this, no,' he retorted. 'Which is why I'm taking you home.'

The word mocked her enough to make her lips curve into an empty smile. 'Home?' she questioned, and for the first time a trace of bitterness crept into her voice. 'You're going to have a bit of a problem with that one. Because I don't have a home. Not any more.'

Kulal leaned over her, only just managing to avoid the arms which were reaching up in an attempt to snake themselves around his neck. He wasn't interested in this particular alcohol-fuelled sob story. He just needed to get rid of her and he needed to do it quickly. 'Where are you staying?' he questioned urgently.

At this, her eyes snapped open and, blurrily, she looked up at him. She tried to sit up, but somehow the effort of moving was just too much. And he had brought her attention to a much bigger problem. Where *was* she staying?

'I've no idea,' she mumbled, tucking her legs underneath her. It was comfortable here and she didn't want to go anywhere else. She wanted to stay with this man with the dark face and glittering eyes because he made her feel safe and he made her feel excited. She gave a luxurious yawn as she snuggled down against the soft leather seat. 'So I guess I'd better stay with you.'

CHAPTER TWO

WARM SUNLIGHT FLOODED over Rosa's face and for a moment she wriggled, reluctant to leave the hypnotic dream which felt curiously realistic.

'I know you're awake.'

The hard, accented voice crashed into her dream and shattered it—even though it was the voice of the man who was responsible for the erotic images which had punctured her restless night.

Her throat feeling as dry as a summer beach, Rosa opened her eyes to find a pair of black eyes trained on her, but there was no lazy speculation or flirtation in them this morning. All she could read was anger and... She cringed. Yes, that was definitely contempt she could see flickering in their ebony depths.

Woozily, she looked around her in an attempt to get her bearings as she tried to piece together the jigsaw memories of last night. Her head was pounding and her mouth felt dry and claggy and she had the feeling that something was very wrong.

Something was. She stared down at herself in horror as she realised that she was in a very large bed—and she was completely naked!

Clutching the fine linen sheet to conceal the jiggle of her breasts, she sat up and stared at the man she knew only as Kulal, who was standing glaring at her from the end of the bed, looking like some kind of dark and avenging angel.

'What happened?' she demanded.

'You don't remember?'

'If I remembered, I wouldn't be asking—would I?'

The disdainful twist of his mouth deepened. 'You want to know if we had sex?'

Rosa felt her cheeks grow hot as she stared at him, appalled by his crude question. But beneath her horror beat the memory of how good it had been to have been held by him on the dance floor and she could feel an unwanted tingling in her breasts. She felt as if she'd left one nightmare and woken up in a different one—and she was going to have to be strong if she wanted to get out of this with any degree of dignity. And she could be strong. She'd proved that, hadn't she? She had survived her mother screaming vitriol at her as she'd made her vile confession. And she'd faced the unbelievable and heartbreaking truth, that her beloved father—the single rock in her life—was not her father at all.

She prayed for the right amount of bravado as she stared into Kulal's furious face. 'And did we?'

At this, he smiled, and it was the coldest smile that Rosa had ever seen.

'Believe me, *garbuua*—if you'd had sex with me, you'd remember it, no matter how drunk you were.'

Rosa met the mocking expression in his eyes, telling herself that she wasn't going to be intimidated. She just needed to extricate herself from this regrettable situation—but first of all she must face facts.

'So we didn't?' she questioned flatly.

'No.'

She held the sheet a little tighter. 'Then how come I'm not wearing any clothes?'

'Because I undressed you.'

'You…undressed me? Why?'

'Why do you think?' he snapped. 'Because I wanted to feast my eyes on your delectable body?' And yet Kulal felt the sudden fierce beat of his heart as he tried to subdue the memory of her firm flesh as he had stripped her bare. He'd taken her clothes off on autopilot, averting his eyes when he had slithered that wispy little pair of lace panties down over her knees. In her uninhibited state she had grabbed him and pulled him down towards her—and he'd had the tantalising experience of having his head buried in her magnificent breasts before he had forced himself to move his aching body away. 'If you must know, I removed your clothes because I didn't think you'd want to leave here this morning wearing last night's crumpled dress, or underwear.'

The gap in her memory was making Rosa feel frightened but she wasn't going to let him know that. 'Is that so?' she said.

Kulal heard the disbelief in her voice and felt a slow anger begin to simmer inside him. Didn't she realise how lucky she'd been that someone like him had been the man she'd targeted last night? That somebody completely lacking in moral scruples could have taken her home and… His mouth hardened. 'I'll tell you exactly what happened,' he bit out. 'You couldn't remember where you were staying, and just before you passed out on the back seat of my limousine, you announced that you wanted to stay with me.'

Rosa could do absolutely nothing about the blush which stained her cheeks. 'I said that?'

'You did,' he agreed grimly. 'Leaving me with little choice other than to bring you back here to my hotel. My plan was to get you inside as quietly and as unobtrusively as possible—but unfortunately, that was not on your agenda.'

She saw the furious accusation which had darkened his face. 'It wasn't?' she questioned as a trace of nerves began to creep into her voice.

'Indeed it wasn't. You decided that as many of the people in the immediate vicinity and beyond should know exactly what you wanted—and what you wanted was to go down to the beach and look at the sky....'

Oh, God. It was all coming back to her now. He'd promised to take her somewhere to look at the stars. He'd said that to her in the nightclub as he'd held her in his arms. And in that moment, she felt as if he'd been offering her a slice of paradise. 'What...what happened?' she whispered.

'I decided that an excess of alcohol, a senseless female and close proximity to the Mediterranean were a potentially lethal combination and so I carried you in here, undressed you—and put you to bed.'

'And that's it?'

'That's it.'

'So where did you sleep?' she questioned pointedly.

He gave a short laugh. 'When you rent a hotel villa overlooking the Mediterranean, there tends to be more than one bedroom. In fact, there are three—so I slept in the one next door.'

Rosa's mind was spinning as she listened to his explanation, but the one thought which was uppermost was that her virtue was still intact—and that surprised her. Because she did remember the heady rush of abandonment she'd felt as he'd held her on the dance floor. She wasn't experienced, but she didn't need to be to realise that she'd been putty in his hands last night. That if he hadn't been so moral, then he would have been lying beside her now. Because she had wanted him. Come to think of it, she still wanted him.

He had moved away from the bed and now that he was at a distance it gave her a better opportunity to study him. She wondered where he was from—his rich accent certainly didn't sound Mediterranean and his skin was much too dark.

'Who are you?' she questioned suddenly.

Kulal tensed, realising that he had been expecting this question a whole lot sooner and knowing that his answer would bring with it a whole new set of baggage. Should he lie? Adopt some fictitious identity, knowing that their paths would never cross again? But that might add fuel to a possibly combustive situation. She had already humiliated herself through her drunken behaviour—if she then discovered that he was lying to her, then mightn't she take out her shame on him? He knew women well enough to know that they were impossible when you rejected them. So why not keep her sweet? Why not make her appreciate just how much he had done for her?

'My name is Kulal,' he said.

'I already know that bit. Where are you from—you're not Mediterranean, are you?'

'No, I am not. I come from a country called Zahrastan.' He searched her face for signs of recognition. 'Any idea where that is?'

She shrugged. 'I'm afraid I've never heard of it. Should I have done?'

Kulal told himself that he shouldn't have been surprised. He wouldn't really expect a pole-dancing socialite to know much about the Arabian principality which produced a vast tranche of the world's oil supply, would he? She probably thought of little else other than which colour she was going to paint her pretty little toenails each day. 'I suggest you try acquainting yourself with a map of the world if you want to find out its exact position.' His voice was dismissive as he slanted her a cool look. 'Now, have I answered all your questions to your satisfaction?'

She wanted to say that no, he hadn't. She wanted to ask him if they couldn't just forget about the disastrous way the evening had ended. If only it was possible to rewind life and stop at the bit you liked best. When she'd been dancing with him it had all felt so…promising. But the repressive note in his voice and the unwelcoming look on his face made her realise that this was not a conversation he was keen on extending. She lifted her fingertips to her temples as if that might help reduce the pounding inside her skull, but it didn't.

'My head hurts,' she said, painfully aware that the first and last hangover of her life should have been conducted in front of such a critical audience.

Kulal nodded as he saw an acceptable exit sign looming ahead. 'So why don't you get showered and dressed?' he suggested smoothly. 'Your things are hanging up in the bathroom and I can order you something to eat. You'll feel much better once you've had some breakfast—'

'I don't want any breakfast,' she snapped, realising that he couldn't wait to get rid of her.

'You ought to. When did you last eat?'

She shook her head. 'I don't remember.'

Reluctantly, he found his gaze drawn to her eyes which had been illuminated by the bright sunshine, and for the first time he noticed that their darkness was broken by flecks of green and gold which made him think of the filtered sunlight you sometimes found in a quiet forest glade. But despite their natural beauty, there was no disguising the shadows which lay beneath them—shadows which were not caused simply by her smudged mascara. Her eyes looked empty, he realised—as if she had seen something which had haunted her. And she was pale. Very pale. Beneath that smooth olive skin of hers, she had the pinched look of a woman who had stopped caring—not about her appearance, but about life itself.

And that was not his business.

He was a royal prince and he was about to announce his engagement to a royal princess. The last thing he needed was to start worrying about the welfare of some spoiled little rich girl who had got herself plastered. Thank God he'd been strong enough to walk away from the promise of her amazing body—he should start being grateful for the lucky escape he'd had.

But something was nagging at his conscience and he found himself unable to ignore it.

'You're not leaving here until you've eaten something,' he said forcefully.

'And you'd be prepared to stop me, would you?'

He raised his eyebrows. 'I don't intend to pick you up for a second time if you pass out and I don't want the drama of a French ambulance screaming to a halt outside. So why don't you do something sensible for the first time in your life and eat something?' he said, turning on his heel and heading for the door.

Rosa stood watching as the door banged shut behind him and she could have burst into howls of frustration. How dare he judge her and find her wanting—when last night he hadn't been able to keep his hands off her?

He could do anything he liked, she realised, because she had put herself in a position to be judged. Angrily, she pushed aside the sheet and headed for the bathroom, recoiling as she caught sight of her reflection in the huge mirror. It was a shock on so many levels, because walking around naked wasn't something she ever did. In Sicily, she always wore a silk nightgown to preserve her modesty because that was how she'd been brought up.

'Imagine if there was a fire in the middle of the night,' her mother had once said, in that tart way she had of speaking to her only daughter. 'And the fireman found you naked and indecent. That is not the way a lady behaves, Rosa.'

As she stood beneath the torrential jets of the shower, Rosa's lips curved with derision. She had just accepted her mother's opinion, hadn't she? The way she always did. Never realising that the woman who had brought her up so strictly was nothing but a cheating hypocrite.

Quickly, she turned on the cold tap—hoping that the shock of the icy water might wash away the memories of the past few days, but it wasn't easy to forget her mother's dramatic confession. She stayed in the shower until she had scrubbed herself clean, and afterwards she found an unused toothbrush and paste and located her clothes and hairbrush. By the time she heard a knock on the bedroom door, she felt a million times better and she psyched herself up to face the judgemental face of Kulal.

'Come in,' she said crisply, her heart beginning to race as he walked in. 'I'm ready.'

'So I see,' Kulal said, reluctantly letting his gaze drift over her. Her feet were bare and the crimson minidress brushed the smooth skin of her thighs. For a moment he felt a powerful wave of temptation as he imagined taking her back to bed, before he swatted it away. She was trouble, he told himself. Last night, he might have been swayed by her beauty and her dancing, but in the cold light of day he knew she was best avoided.

'I've ordered breakfast to be served on the terrace,' he said. 'So why don't we go downstairs?'

Hunger made Rosa nod her head in grudging agreement and she followed him down a wide marble staircase and out onto a terrace, where a table had been laid with croissants, juices and jams, and what looked like a dish of iced mango. The terrace overlooked landscaped gardens and, in the distance, she caught a glimpse of the sapphire sea. It felt as if they were in a self-contained world of their own—a private little bubble which was miles away from the hustle and bustle of the French Riviera. 'Did you say this was a hotel?' she asked curiously.

'It is, but I always rent one of the two villas which are attached to it. They come with their own gardens and that affords me more privacy.'

Rosa sank into one of the wicker chairs and looked up into the flatness of his eyes. 'Which makes it easier to get rid of unwanted overnight guests in the morning, I suppose?'

He sat down opposite her—a movement which immediately heralded the appearance of a butler bearing a large silver pot of coffee. Let her know exactly where she stands, Kulal told himself. Tell her the truth, even if the truth hurts. 'That is always a consideration to take into account,' he agreed.

Rosa stared at the inky coffee which was being poured for her before Kulal waved the butler away. She wasn't going to cause a scene about what he'd just said, when all he'd done was be honest. It would have been much worse if he'd pretended otherwise—if he made out that he'd never taken a strange woman back to his hotel before. And wasn't she all done with lies and subterfuge? 'Wise man,' she said lightly.

Her casual tone made Kulal relax and he sat back in his chair. So she was going to behave herself, was she? He guessed she must have done this kind of thing plenty of times herself. The slightly stilted morning breakfast after a night of red-hot sex.

His mouth hardened as he forced himself to face the frustrating and rather laughable truth. Because you haven't actually had sex with her, have you?

He watched as she pulled a croissant from the bread basket and began to cover it in strawberry jam. With her dark hair drying in the sunshine and her body smelling of soap rather than perfume, he thought how different she looked this morning. Her face was completely bare of make-up so that she looked very young and almost innocent. Her pink lips were so delicious that it seemed a crime not to lean across the table and kiss them, and for a split second he imagined his tongue licking its way inside her mouth. Until he remembered the way she'd been writhing her hips around the pole last night and forced himself to dampen down his ardour. What chameleons women were, he thought. How they changed faster than the seasons! She was about as innocent as one of the houris who charged men by the hour for their services.

Even so, as he watched her lift a glass of *jus de pamplemousse* to her lips, he couldn't ignore the undeniable regret that he hadn't made love to her. Because she would be an amazing lover. The sexual connoisseur in him told him that—even if he hadn't witnessed the sensational way she'd been moving on the podium last night. As he'd put her to bed, her beauty had been revealed to him in all its shockingly sensual glory. He had felt deliciously firm skin as he'd peeled the little dress from her body. And it had taken more strength than he'd ever needed to walk away and spend a restless night in the bed next door.

He waited until she'd finished eating, until she had dabbed those delectable lips with a napkin, before putting down his own coffee cup and subjecting her to a steady stare. 'I'm assuming that by now you've remembered where you're staying?'

Rosa winced. What would he say if she told him that she'd never been drunk like that before? That she'd just discovered that her mother had cheated with her husband's own brother—and her whole world had been smashed apart?

How would he react? Well, he might believe her or he might not, but that would make no difference to the fact that he couldn't wait to get rid of her.

'I'm staying at the Hotel Jasmin,' she said, getting to her feet. 'So if you wouldn't mind calling me a cab, I'll get out of your way.'

Kulal rose from the wicker chair, knowing that he could easily send her home in his own car, but it was a pretty distinctive car and it would inevitably connect them. This part of the Riviera was always crawling with paparazzi, eager to capture the indiscretions of celebrities. They'd been lucky enough not to have been seen last night when he'd had to carry her inside—so maybe he should count his blessings and get rid of her as anonymously as possible.

'I'll get reception to organise it for you,' he said. 'And arrange for someone to show you through to the main part of the hotel.'

Rosa felt like a piece of garbage which was headed

for the recycling bin and wondered if it was possible to feel any worse than she did right then. She was never going to touch another drop of alcohol in her life! And she was never going to dance with dark and danger-ous-looking strangers in nightclubs. She nodded as she looked up into his black eyes, unprepared for his sud-den movement as he touched her hair before running his fingertips lightly down the side of her face in a gesture which felt almost gentle.

'Just do yourself a favour, will you?' he said roughly. 'And stay off the booze in future.'

His words affected her far more than they should have done and Rosa recognised how lucky she'd been in her choice of rescuer. He had plucked her from the sweaty scrum in the nightclub and danced with her, and then she had blown it. She had got drunk and passed out but he hadn't taken advantage of her sorry state, even though it would have been easy for him to do so. And if he was clearly appalled by her behaviour—well, who could blame him? She was pretty appalled by it her-self and she'd never get another chance to show him that deep down she wasn't really like that. Worst of all was that she would never know what it was like to kiss him....

The old Rosa might have slunk off—but of course the old Rosa would never have found herself in such a compromising position. And the new Rosa wanted to have a taste of pleasure—just one—before she walked out of his life for good.

She stood up on tiptoe and framed her hands around his hard jaw before leaning forward to brush her lips over the sensual curve of his mouth. 'Thank you,' she whispered. 'For your hospitality and your chivalry.'

For a moment he didn't move and it was as if her soft words had turned him to stone. Rosa could see a little muscle working overtime at his temple before he drawled out a sardonic reply. 'I'd like to say that the pleasure was all mine, but that wouldn't be true.'

She looked at him uncertainly. 'No?'

'In fact, it was an evening which fell pretty short on the pleasure quota for both of us, and I'm wondering whether it might not be too late to remedy that....'

Rosa was unprepared for the decisive way that he pulled her against him and the equally decisive way that he drove his mouth down onto hers. His hands were cupping her head and her hair was spilling through his fingers and suddenly he was kissing her like she'd never been kissed before. She could feel the instant flowering of her breasts and a delicious warmth between her legs. Did he know that? Was that why he thrust one hard thigh between hers, as if sensing that might help alleviate the sudden aching she could feel at the most intimate part of her body?

'Oh,' she said against his lips, swallowing down her sense of wonder. 'Oh.'

With an effort, he tore his lips away and looked down into her upturned face. 'How commendably circumspect I have been with you, my beauty,' he said shakily. 'But that all ends as of now. You are no longer drunk and I am no longer angry. This may be one of the most ill-judged decisions of my life, but I want you—and, sweet heaven, I am going to have you. Right now.'

His emphatic statement should have daunted her, but it didn't. She suspected that he didn't particularly like or respect her, but suddenly Rosa didn't care. She didn't care about anything other than the way he was making her feel. Why shouldn't she taste the pleasures which seemed to drive everyone else in the human race, except for her—poor, protected Rosa, who had been shielded from the world for so long? Her lips were dry but somehow she managed to echo his words as she felt his thumb tease its way over one painfully erect nipple.

'I want you, too,' she whispered. 'And right now is fine with me.'

With a hard smile of satisfaction, he bent his head to kiss her again and Rosa never knew what would have happened next had she not heard the sound of an embarrassed cough behind them. With a start, they sprang apart—as if they'd been caught red-handed at the scene of a crime.

And maybe they had, she thought. Because there, standing at the edge of the private garden watching them, was a man as dark-skinned as Kulal himself, though his head was dipped with the faintest degree of subservience.

She watched as a look of anger darkened Kulal's face. 'What the hell is going on?' he demanded. 'Why the hell are you disturbing me, Mutasim—creeping up on me like a spy?'

Rosa thought she'd never seen a man look more embarrassed than Mutasim did as Kulal's words fired into him, and she noticed that the stranger hadn't met her eyes. Not once.

'I beg your indulgence at this untimely intrusion, Your Highness,' said Mutasim softly. 'But your brother, the king, craves your company at the earliest opportunity.'

Rosa's lips parted in shock as the words registered in her befuddled brain. She looked up at Kulal, her bewildered eyes asking him a silent question.

Highness? King?

Were they playing some sort of joke on her? Talking in some kind of code? But her confusion was quickly superseded by shame as Kulal took no notice of her silent plea. Completely ignoring her, he walked over to the dark-skinned man and began to speak in a low voice, in a language she couldn't begin to understand.

And Rosa felt completely invisible.

CHAPTER THREE

'So what did you think you were playing at, Kulal?'
The king was shaking his head in disbelief. 'When you
decided to take some drunken pole dancer back to your
hotel?'

For a moment Kulal didn't answer. Instead he sat
back in one of the ornate chairs in the throne room and
stared up at the old-fashioned fan which was whirring
in the vaulted, golden ceiling. He was back in the ancient palace in which he'd been raised, having flown
to Zahrastan as soon as he had received word that the
king wished to speak with him. He'd never received a
summons quite like this and it occurred to him that he'd
never seen his brother look quite so exasperated either.
Not even during that time when he had caught Kulal
leaving one of the chambermaid's rooms, smoothing
down his ruffled robes and smirking all over his face.

Or the time when Kulal had 'borrowed' one of the
palace cars for an unauthorised trip into the desert when
he was barely sixteen and nobody had known that he
could drive. On both those occasions—and, indeed, on
many more—righteous anger should surely have come
flooding the younger prince's way, but it had not. It was

almost as if it had been expected that he should behave wildly—and everyone knew why. Weren't motherless children always indulged?

As two royal princes of a fabulously rich desert kingdom, the two men should have been close but an accident of birth meant that they had grown up living two very different lives. Hazail was the older, the heir to the throne, and the defining factor of his life had always been that he would one day inherit the crown. It had been Hazail's destiny which had occupied most of their father's time as he had tutored his elder son in the art of ruling a powerful desert kingdom.

Kulal had simply been the 'spare'—the extra boy child born as an insurance policy to ensure the line of succession. He had been brought up by a series of amahs—female servants who had adored him but had lacked the strength to discipline the strong-minded little boy. Consequently, he had been given freedom—perhaps a little too much freedom for so strong and so wilful a character. But that had never compensated for the heavy weight which had hung over him since his mother had died—a shocking death which had sent the country spiralling into deep mourning. And Kulal had been marked out by that terrible loss, for she had died saving his life. Deep down he knew that was the reason why his father and his brother had always been so distant towards him. He knew that subconsciously they blamed him for the queen's untimely end, even if logic told him that it was nothing but the cruel intervention of fate. Of two people being in the wrong place at the wrong time.

Perhaps it had been to make up for their emotional distance that they had tended to overlook Kulal's misdemeanours. But it seemed that they were not being overlooked this time. Hazail was pacing the floor like an expectant father, before turning back to his younger brother, still with that exasperated expression on his face.

'She wasn't a pole dancer,' Kulal protested as he picked up a golden goblet and swirled the pomegranate juice it contained.

'No?' Hazail looked at him. 'It is fiction, then, that she was seen writhing around in a nightclub, showing much of her underwear in the process? That is simply a figment of my informant's imagination, is it?'

'Which informant?' Kulal demanded, trying to dampen down the vivid image of Rosa's curvaceous body as it had twisted itself around the pole. Or the fact that his brother's damned servant had interrupted him just as he had started to seduce her!

'That is surely beside the point,' answered Hazail coolly. 'Unless you're denying that you took this exhibitionist back to your hotel with you?'

Kulal shrugged. 'No, I am not denying it.'

'She seems a little outré even for your extravagant tastes, Kulal.'

'I know.' Kulal met the question in his brother's eyes with a faintly bemused shrug, because he couldn't have begun to describe the sensation which had washed over him when he'd watched Rosa walk into the nightclub that night. Lust didn't begin to cover the hunger he'd felt when he'd seen her. There had been something in her eyes—a look which had seemed so at odds with the provocative curves of her body and which had called out to something inside him. He had noticed the defiant way she'd lifted the champagne bottle to her mouth and the small rush of foam which had trickled erotically over her lips. And then she had begun to dance....

Kulal felt desire shiver over his skin as he remembered that dance. It had been an invitation to sex. The most blatant and beautiful invitation he had ever witnessed and he had simply been unable to resist it. He had walked towards her like a man on autopilot, with his heart thundering and his body on fire. 'But she is very beautiful,' he said simply.

'There are a lot of beautiful women in the world, as well you know,' came Hazail's dry rejoinder. 'Surely you could have found someone a little more suitable to have sex with?'

Kulal wanted to protest that they hadn't actually had sex, but his fiercely masculine pride would not allow him to make such a disclosure, especially not to his brother. 'I'm not really clear about why there has been a big drama about it, Hazail?' he drawled. 'Why the sudden interest in my sex life?'

'Because you are engaged to be married—in case it had slipped your mind. And therefore it is inadvisable for you to behave like a rutting stag!'

Kulal thought of his serious-faced fiancée—a blue-blooded princess who hailed from the neighbouring country of Buheiraat. He thought about the matter-of-fact way the two of them had sat down to work out an agreement for their forthcoming nuptials. He thought about her complete lack of passion and compared her to the fiery and responsive Rosa, and his heart sank.

He shot his brother a cool look. 'I made a single, minor transgression, Hazail,' he said. 'I hardly think that puts me in the category of "rutting stag." And besides, you know how these things work. Ayesha will not be expecting her prince to come to her on her wedding night as a cowering innocent. She will expect her husband to be experienced in matters of sexuality.'

'Well, Ayesha's expectations are now academic,' said Hazail. 'Since the wedding is now off.'

Kulal stilled. 'The wedding is off?'

'Yes. She has sent word to the palace through one of her envoys that she will no longer marry you.'

Kulal's eyes narrowed. 'Why not?'

'Why do you think?' exploded Hazail. 'Because word has got back to her about your exploits, that's why! You seem to forget that modern princesses are different to the way they used to be. They are no longer prepared to turn a blind eye to behaviour which they find intolerable. And you have hardly been the soul of discretion on this occasion, Kulal. A discreet liaison is one thing, but openly spending the night with a complete stranger is something else.'

Kulal's mouth hardened because it had been the loud and drunken Rosa who had made it into such a spectacle. If she hadn't been so damned predatory, this might never have happened. He glowered at his golden goblet and slammed it down on the table. 'I will write to Ayesha, wishing her all the very best for her future happiness,' he said. 'And we will forget that this unfortunate incident ever happened.'

But Hazail was shaking his head. 'That's the trouble—we can't just forget it. If only it were that simple.'

Kulal frowned. 'You're not making any sense.'

The king leaned back in his chair. 'You do realise the identity of the woman you spent the night with?'

'Of course I do.' Kulal felt a beat of frustration harden his groin, his erection conveniently concealed by the silk robes he always wore when in Zahrastan. And although it felt like an exquisite form of torture, he allowed a picture of her luscious curves and dark hair to form in his mind. 'Her name is Rosa.'

'Her name is Rosa Corretti!'

Kulal's expression remained unchanged, for he did not care to admit that the brunette's surname was news to him. 'Mmm. That's right. Corretti. She's Italian,' he said, as if imparting some important nugget of information.

'No, she is not Italian,' said Hazail. 'She's Sicilian. And not only is she Sicilian, but she comes from one of the most powerful families on the island.'

'So?'

'So her brothers are probably going to come after you. In fact, the whole damned family is probably going to come after you after you compromised her reputation by spending the night with her.'

Kulal shrugged. 'Then let them come,' he said carelessly. 'For I am afraid of no man!'

'Your courage has never been in question, but you don't seem to realise the gravity of the situation, Kulal.'

Hazail bit his lip with the closest thing to anxiety Kulal had ever seen. 'The influence of the Corretti family extends all over the world and they do not take the virtue of their womenfolk lightly. I'm not joking—this could be political and economic dynamite for our country if it were to erupt into some kind of international scandal.'

There was silence for a moment as Kulal mulled over his brother's words. Were this Corretti family such a big deal, then? He remembered everything he had heard and read about the Sicilian culture. That the men were proud and the women were pure. His lips twisted scornfully. Except that Rosa Corretti was the least pure woman he'd met in a long time!

'Do you think they might respond to bribery?' he mused. 'Shares in one of our oil refineries might buy their silence.'

Hazail shook his head. 'This is one situation where I suspect that bribery will not work—for there are very few ways to appease a Sicilian family when their honour is involved.'

For a moment, Kulal was silent as he considered the options which lay open to him and forced himself to acknowledge that there were remarkably few. He thought about Rosa Corretti and her soft pink lips. He thought about her magnificent breasts and waterfall of dark hair and he felt a corresponding pang of pure and frustrated lust. Surely there was something he could do to remedy a potentially explosive situation?

And then an idea began to form in his mind, an idea so simple that he was surprised it had taken him so long to come up with it.

'I suppose I will have to marry her,' he said.

Hazail stared at him. 'Marry her?'

Kulal shrugged. 'Why not? A short-term marriage would suit both parties very well. It would rescue her "honour," silence any overprotective brothers and it might work in our favour. Think about it, Hazail. We sell the story as some kind of love match and Princess Ayesha will be seen as magnanimous for agreeing to cancel her wedding to me. And just think how the press will seize on it!' He gave a mocking smile. 'The Arabian version of Romeo and Juliet!'

The king's mouth fell open. 'You're serious, aren't you?'

'Entirely serious.' Kulal smiled as he allowed his body to anticipate the pleasure of reuniting with his little Sicilian firecracker. 'I shall go to Rosa Corretti and ask for her hand in marriage.'

There was a pause as the king looked at him. 'This is remarkably good of you, Kulal,' he said quietly.

'Ah, but I am not doing it to be "good,"' Kulal corrected silkily. 'I am doing it because I can see no feasible alternative. Look on it as an act of supreme patriotism, if you will. Let's just say I'm doing it for the sake of my country.'

CHAPTER FOUR

Rosa had been crossing the room towards the bathroom when the sudden rap on the door halted her in her tracks. She could feel a sudden clamminess on her forehead and her heart began to pound with something which felt very much like fear. Who on earth was that knocking at this time of night? She wasn't expecting any visitors and this wasn't the kind of hotel which offered room service. More importantly, nobody knew she was here.

Or at least, only one person did and she doubted she'd ever see him again.

But her heart began to race as a series of ghastly possibilities began to crowd into her mind. What if Kulal wasn't the only person who knew of her whereabouts? What if her brothers who she must now refer to as her half-brothers had discovered she was here? They might have been horrified to find out that she didn't share their father—and that their mother had brought shame and disgrace to the family with her behaviour. Their eyes may have deadened with anger on discovering that she was not their true blood sister, but surely twenty-three years of guarding her as fiercely as a lion might guard its cubs could not be forgotten overnight?

Mightn't they have decided to bring her back to Sicily themselves? Wasn't that the gist behind the text which she'd received? The one which had simply said, Come home, Rosa.

She had ignored the text, just as she had ignored the one which had followed shortly after. In fact, she'd hurled the phone at the wall so that it had fallen in shattered and useless pieces on the carpet. But she planned to get herself a new, cheap one tomorrow morning and then none of the Correttis would have her new number. Which meant that none of them would be able to contact her.

And in the meantime, why was someone still knocking on her door like that?

She stayed rooted to the spot, praying that it was a case of mistaken identity. A drunken reveller, perhaps—for there were enough of them in this part of the South of France. She felt her skin redden. Because hadn't she been one of those drunken revellers herself the other night, when she'd made such an awful fool of herself in front of that arrogant man, Kulal? It was ironic, really. She'd grown up surrounded by arrogant men and seen the heartbreak they could wreak on women, so why hadn't she chosen someone softer and easier as the man she had decided she wanted to take her virginity?

Briefly she shut her eyes because the most humiliating thing of all was that he hadn't wanted her. He'd put her to bed after too much champagne and the disdain on his face the following morning had been clear. It was only when she'd practically thrown herself at him that he had deigned to kiss her. She wondered if they would have gone all the way had the kiss not been interrupted by that other man, the one who'd started talking about a king.

She still couldn't quite believe the words he'd uttered. Something about the king 'craving his company.' Did people really talk like that any more? Perhaps they were some kind of double act who trawled holiday areas pretending to be people they weren't. Operating some kind of cheap scam.

'I know you're in there.'

The terse words carried through the closed door and put a swift halt to Rosa's swirling thoughts. Because that deep voice with the strange accent was horribly familiar and she was unprepared for the wave of desire which made her skin grow heated. A curling expectation began to unfold somewhere deep inside her and it wasn't a feeling she particularly welcomed. She thought of his cruel face and hard body and her heart began to pound. What was the matter with her? He was probably nothing but a weird imposter—some fake sheikh—and she didn't have to answer the door to him.

Oh, why hadn't she turned the lights off?

Because you weren't expecting a late-night visitor, that's why.

'You can try ignoring me if you want, Rosa, but I'm not going anywhere,' persisted the voice. 'And if you stretch my patience too far, then I may be forced to break down this door.'

What a caveman he was! Rosa racked her brain for some kind of response and decided to attempt an audacious piece of bravado. 'And what if I'm not alone?' she demanded. 'Don't you think you might be disturbing something—that I might want a little privacy?'

From the other side of the door, Kulal gritted his teeth as a slow rage began to build inside him. Bad enough that he was being forced to enter a union with this tramp of a woman, but that she should dare to keep him waiting was intolerable!

'Then I'd advise you to tell your paramour to get dressed and to get dressed quickly, since he might not enjoy facing me in my current mood.'

Rosa shivered at the forceful intent behind his words. She should have been shocked by his arrogance, but she was Sicilian and therefore she wasn't a bit shocked. She was used to outrageously chauvinist behaviour within the Corretti clan itself, but this man was making the male members of her own overbearing family seem like absolute pussycats.

Reluctantly, she unlocked the key and opened the door, her senses assailed by the overpowering scent of jasmine from the darkened gardens as she stared at the man who was standing on her doorstep.

He was exactly as she remembered him. No, that wasn't quite true. She'd spent the past two days trying to play him down in her imagination, telling herself that it had been her highly emotional state which had made her react to him in such an uncharacteristic way. Telling herself that he was nothing special, that he was just a man who was aware of his appeal to women and who played on it.

But she had been wrong. More than wrong. Because tonight, his undeniable sexiness was edged with something potent—something which suddenly made her feel innocent and fragile. He looked as if he meant business—and it wasn't just the way he was dressed, in a dark and sombre suit, which emphasised his powerful physique. He looked as if he hadn't shaved that day so that his dark jaw was faintly shadowed with stubble. It was a look which was essentially masculine and subtly modern, yet it didn't match the expression in his black eyes. Because that was the antithesis of modern—it was darkly glittering and almost primitive.

She swallowed. 'What do you want?'

'A little courtesy might be a good place to start. I'd like to come in.'

To Rosa's disbelief he didn't bother waiting for her assent, just walked straight past her. 'You can't just barge in here like that!' she protested.

'Too late. I just did. So let's not waste any more time with futile protestations. Shut the door like a good girl, will you? I want to talk to you.'

Fury came in many forms and the form which was visiting Rosa right then was making her speechless with a growing anger. Like a good girl, he had said—and hadn't she run away from Sicily to escape precisely that type of patronising attitude? It took a moment or two before she could compose herself enough to suck in a deep breath and manage to turn it into an outraged question.

'What are you doing here?' she demanded.

'Are you going to shut the door, or am I?'

She kicked it shut before she could ask herself why she wasn't calling hotel security—if such a thing existed in this place—to have him ejected. Maybe because there seemed something distinctly unfinished between them—something which still needed to be said. But she wasn't going to let him think that she was a pushover, even though her heart was now racing for a very different reason. She had behaved like a stupid fool the other night and she didn't intend to do so again. 'I didn't think we had anything left to say to each other, after that man Mutasim bundled me into a taxi the other day.'

He didn't appear to be listening to her for his eyes were trained on the closed door in the far corner of the room. 'So is there some thwarted lover in there?' he questioned softly. 'Cowering in fear as he puts his clothes back on?'

For a moment Rosa was tempted to say yes, wondering if he would have the bravado to actually go in and confront some fictitious man. But deep down she knew the answer. Of course he would. She could tell from the tension in his powerful body that he was afraid of nothing. Or no one.

But then, neither was she, she reminded herself. Not any more. She'd spent her whole life being bossed around by autocratic men and being reined in by old-fashioned rules, and the new Rosa Corretti had no intention of continuing with that repressive tradition. So this Kulal—whoever he was—had better understand that, before she kicked him out of here for good.

'No, I haven't got anyone cowering in the bedroom—not that it's any of your business if I had,' she snapped. 'I was about to go to bed myself when I was rudely interrupted by your unwanted appearance.'

Kulal felt his pulse quicken. So she was alone, was

she? Alone and probably as hungry for him as she'd been the other night. And wouldn't that be the easiest way to get her to agree to his proposition—by getting her horizontal? His lips curved with the hint of an expectant smile. Because a woman would agree to pretty much anything when a man was making love to her.

Now that he was safely in her hotel room, he allowed himself to study her closely—thinking that she looked very different to the sexy strumpet who had writhed around the pole in her tiny crimson dress the other night. Her dark hair was tied over one shoulder in a single plait and she wore a heavy, silken robe, which shimmered to the ground as she moved. A classy kind of garment, he thought approvingly. And even though it covered every inch of her body, the delicate fabric still clung to every delicious curve, reminding him all too vividly of what lay beneath.

'You are looking very beautiful tonight,' he murmured.

Rosa stiffened because the calculating look she'd seen hardening his eyes was completely at odds with the silken caress of his voice. And yet stupidly, her body couldn't seem to stop reacting to him. She wanted him to pull her into his hard body and she wanted him to kiss her again. But he was trouble. She knew that. He might exude an undeniable appeal which was clawing away at something deep inside her, but she sensed an undeniable danger about him.

'I asked what you were doing here,' she said quietly. 'And so far you haven't come up with a satisfactory answer.'

Kulal frowned. She was certainly behaving very differently this evening. She wasn't coming on to him at all, or making any indication that she wanted to continue the delicious kiss which had been abruptly terminated by the appearance of his brother's aide.

'We need to have a conversation,' he said.

'At this time of night?'

He nodded. The concealing cloak of nighttime was infinitely preferable to a meeting conducted in the harsh light of the Mediterranean sunshine. And even though this rather humble hotel was not the kind of place which usually attracted the paparazzi, his striking looks always made him the subject of prying eyes. 'I'm afraid so.'

'Then you'd better hurry up and get on with it, Mr...?'

He met the challenge in her voice, thinking how spectacular her eyes were, as they looked at him with impertinent challenge. 'I think you were made perfectly aware by the interruption which took place yesterday that I am not a "Mr,"' he said shortly. 'In fact, I am a prince.'

'A prince?' she echoed, like someone waiting for the punchline to a joke.

He nodded. 'Although I prefer to think of myself as a sheikh first and a prince second. I am Sheikh Kulal Al-Dimashqi, the second son of the royal house of Zahrastan.' He elevated his dark brows in careless question. 'But perhaps you have found out a little more about me since we were parted so abruptly. Was your interest not piqued by the stranger you almost had sex with?' He gave a mocking smile. 'Especially when you discovered that his brother was a king.'

Rosa glared at him, trying to ignore his crude taunt. 'If you must know—I thought that you might be involved in some kind of scam.'

'A scam?' he echoed.

'Yes. That man turning up and announcing that the "king" wanted to see you.' She gave him a scornful look. 'People pretend to be aristocrats all the time! It helps them get into expensive hotels without paying.'

He gave the room a deprecating glance. 'Then I don't imagine they'd be targeting a place like this, do you?'

Rosa didn't rise to the taunt. Why should she, when it was true? She'd chosen the hotel precisely because it hadn't been expensive. Because it was the last place on earth that you would ever expect to find a Corretti staying and therefore it was unlikely that any of her family would come looking for her here. But the Hotel Jasmin was exactly what she needed in her troubled state. She liked the peace of the place. The laid-back attitude and the old-fashioned gardens. There were mostly French people staying here and the service was simple and unobtrusive. There were no tourists, no dull international menu or any Wi-Fi connection which might have encouraged people to sit around, tapping away on their computers so that you felt as if you'd walked into a giant office.

'If you don't like it, then leave,' she said quietly. 'I'm not stopping you.'

Kulal hesitated—and for him, such hesitation was rare. But this conversation was not going according to plan. For a start, she had not fallen on him with lust in her eyes and a body impatient for the pleasure he could give her. He had thought that he would be in her bed by now and yet he was nowhere near it. She seemed completely different to the woman who had begged him to kiss her and he began to wonder why.

'I know who you are,' he said suddenly.

Rosa didn't react. It had been one of the first lessons she had been taught—never show a stranger what you are thinking. She had broken that rule the other night, under the influence of the unaccustomed champagne, but she would not be repeating such a fundamental mistake tonight.

'And who am I?' she questioned lightly, thinking that perhaps he could provide a better answer than any she could come up with. Because she didn't seem to know who she was herself any more.

He sucked in a deep breath. 'Your name is Rosa Corretti and you are a member of the prestigious Sicilian family of that name.'

Rosa nodded. At least he hadn't come out with the usual accusatory stereotype, as people usually did. They discovered that you came from a powerful family with a sometimes questionable past, and assumed that you were all gangsters. Hadn't that been one of the reasons why she'd been so protected during her upbringing—to keep her away from the judgement of the outside world, as well as to protect her innocence?

'Bravo, Sheikh Kulal Al-Dimashqi,' she said softly. 'And what else have you found out about me?'

He stared at her. 'Nothing,' he said, his words edged with frustration.

'Nothing?'

He shook his head. He had some of the best intelligence sources in the world, but when it came to finding out more about the daughter of Carlo Corretti, it seemed that they had come up against a brick wall. There was plenty about her two brothers and a whole bunch of colourful cousins, but Rosa might as well not have existed for all the information they'd been able to provide. 'Absolutely nothing. Oh, I know which schools you went to and that you studied linguistics at the University of Palermo, but other than that, not a thing. No lists of lovers and no recorded misdemeanours. No earlier experimentations with pole dancing. You come from a society which seems expert in keeping secrets,' he observed caustically.

Somehow Rosa suppressed a bitter laugh. He didn't know the half of it. Not just a society which was good at keeping secrets, but a family which was riddled with them. 'I think I would agree with that,' she said coolly.

Kulal was starting to feel confused and it was not a feeling he was used to. Because Rosa Corretti was perplexing him. The other night, her sexuality had shimmered off her half-clothed frame like the bright haloes of light which gleamed around the planet Saturn. But tonight, she seemed proud and untouchable. And why was the daughter of such a wealthy dynasty staying in a humble hotel room like this?

'So what brings you to the French Riviera?' he questioned.

Rosa wondered what he would say if she told him. How he would react if she explained that her identity crisis was very real and not the characteristic angst of some spoiled little rich girl. And for a second she was tempted to tell him. To unburden herself to someone who didn't know the Corretti family, and who didn't particularly care about them. Wouldn't it be liberating to share her terrible story with someone else and to free herself from the resulting poison which had flooded through her veins?

But old habits died hard and Rosa was too well-taught in the art of keeping secrets to dare divulge the darkest one of all to this man who was dominating the small room. She could tell him something, yes—she just could not tell him everything.

'I wanted to get away,' she said, giving a careless shrug of her shoulders as if to add credence to her statement. 'To escape from home and see a little of the world. Lots of women my age do that. It's perfectly normal.'

But a trip to see the world did not tend to make a person look so haunted, Kulal thought. His eyes narrowed. 'So it's a temporary trip?'

'I guess.'

'And when are you planning to go back?'

His question was unexpected and it made her confront what she had been doing her best not to confront. Rosa shuddered. Back to what? To a home she no longer recognised and a family who had changed beyond recognition as the result of a few spilled and deadly words?

'I'm not,' she said forcefully. 'I'm never going back to Sicily!'

CHAPTER FIVE

KULAL WATCHED ROSA closely as she bit out her heart-felt words—more closely than he usually bothered to watch any woman, but by now she was beginning to perplex him. He had seen the play of emotions which had crossed her beautiful face when he'd asked her about her native Sicily. He had seen wariness and fear. Disgust too. Yes, he had definitely seen disgust when she had declared that she was never going back home. Someone more curious might have wondered what had caused such an extreme reaction, but he had never been a man to delve too deeply. He was more interested in the facts than in what lay behind them.

'So you will find employment here?' he mused. 'Or perhaps you are wealthy enough to live comfortably without any need to go out to work?'

If he hadn't hit on such a raw nerve, then Rosa might have told him to keep his intrusive questions to himself. Because there always had been money whenever she'd wanted it and plenty of it too. A trust fund had been put in place for her from the moment she'd been born and she'd been able to access it any time she liked. Sometimes she'd wondered what life might have been like if she'd had to save up in order to buy the latest expensive pair of shoes she'd coveted, but that was something she'd never experienced. At least, not until now. Because quickly following the text summoning her home had come another, informing her that all access to her funds had been frozen. That there was no more money to be had.

She knew exactly what her family were trying to do.

They were trying to force her to go back to Sicily by starving her out!

She'd known that they could be ruthless. She'd seen them dispose of enemies and workers—even husbands and wives—she just hadn't realised that the same ruthlessness could be directed at her.

She stared at Kulal as his question lodged in her mind, suddenly realising that even if she did try to go out to work that her options open to her were very limited. She had a respectable degree in languages, but she wasn't actually trained in anything, was she?

'Actually, I'm not wealthy,' she said. 'Not any more.'

'So what are you going to do?' he persisted.

Frustration made her turn on him again. Was he getting some kind of kick by watching her squirm? 'What I do or I don't do is none of your business.'

'But I could make it my business.'

His tone had softened and instinctively Rosa stiffened, for she suspected that this was a man who didn't really do soft. She looked at him suspiciously. 'Why would you do that?'

'Because I think we could offer each other mutual help in a time of mutual need.'

She looked at him suspiciously. 'I'm not sure I understand.'

He took a step forward, closing some of the space between them, and he saw from the sudden tension in her body that she was acutely aware of that fact. As was he... 'I think you're running from something, Rosa,' he said as he stared down into her big, dark eyes. 'Something or someone. I also think that you're hiding—that you don't want anyone to know you're here. And that you're broke. Or at least, if not broke, then rapidly running out of funds.'

Rosa swallowed because his proximity was making her feel as unsettled as his perception. And how spooky was that, when pretty much everything he'd guessed had been true? Soon after she'd found out that her funds had been frozen, she had sold a bracelet to a second-hand jeweller in nearby Nice, but had received much less for it than she'd been expecting. And wasn't it funny how money didn't seem to go anywhere, especially when you weren't used to living frugally? Especially when she'd blown most of her budget on a tiny crimson dress which had got her into all this trouble.

'Why are you so interested in me?' she whispered.

Kulal's mouth flattened into an uncompromising line. Time to destroy any emerging fantasies which might destabilise what he was about to say. 'I'm not interested in you, *habeebi*,' he said softly. 'But more in what we can offer each other.'

Beneath the slippery fabric of her gown, Rosa felt the prickling of her skin and she wasn't sure if it was excitement or fear. Was he going to suggest that they continue where they'd left off the other day, when they were so rudely interrupted in the garden of his hotel villa? And if he did say that…if he pulled her in his arms and kissed her with the same kind of hungry passion she'd tasted the other day, would she honestly be able to push him away?

The words seemed to be having difficulty leaving her mouth, but she knew she had to say them. 'What kind of offer?'

Kulal's lips curved into a smile of satisfaction as he read the unmistakable signs of sexual desire on her face, and knew he was home and dry.

'My offer of marriage,' he said.

His words echoed around the room and a feeling of unreality began to wash over Rosa as she stared into his black eyes. She tried to wonder what it would be like if he'd made his suggestion with some degree of affection, rather than with that cruel and calculating expression. But she was a Corretti, wasn't she? And therefore ideally equipped to deal with his proposal in the same businesslike way as he'd made it.

'Marry you?' she said drily. 'Don't you have someone more suitable you could ask? Perhaps somebody you've known longer than five minutes, in a relationship which is founded on more than lust and insults?'

Briefly, Kulal thought of Ayesha and wondered whether now was the time to reveal his broken engagement. In terms of getting the Corretti girl to agree to his plan, surely it would be better to keep it secret? But he remembered the bitterness on her face as she'd spoken disparagingly about 'secrets' and figured that she was bound to find out some time. Far better it came from him than from some mischievous news source.

'Actually, I had a fiancée,' he said. 'Until very recently.'

Rosa's eyes narrowed. 'How recently?'

There was a pause. 'Until yesterday.'

The brutal time scale meant that no mental calculations were necessary and she stared at him in disbelief. 'You mean you...you made love to me when you were engaged to another woman?'

He gave a short laugh. 'I don't classify kissing someone who has just hurled themselves into my arms as "making love."'

'You bastard,' she said quietly. 'You complete and utter bastard. You know damned well that if I hadn't been drunk then, you would have ended up in my bed that night.'

Kulal only just managed to repress a shudder. It was outrageous that he was going to have to marry a woman like this. A woman who showed no shame about spreading her favours so widely. Yes, he liked his lovers to be liberated—of course he did—but a wife was something completely different. That a royal prince should take such a tramp as his bride was unthinkable! Until he reminded himself that this was intended to be nothing but a temporary marriage and that her virtue was irrelevant. He remembered the way she'd kissed him. The way she'd pressed her delicious body into his so her magnificent breasts had flattened against his chest. At least she would come to the bridal chamber with a satisfying degree of sexual knowledge.

'I was behaving no differently to how men have always behaved,' he drawled.

'You mean you expected your fiancée to ignore your outrageous behaviour?'

'I expected my fiancée to know nothing about what I was doing,' he said. 'But it seems I was wrong. And it also seems she didn't understand that a man owes it to his future bride to gain as much experience as possible before he takes her innocence on their wedding night.'

Rosa almost laughed at his insolence. 'Is that supposed to be a joke?'

'What's funny about it?'

'You're making it sound as if you were doing her a favour by sleeping with as many women as possible.'

'That is one way of looking at it,' he agreed seriously. 'And it is certainly a valid point. Generations of men from all cultures have taken a comprehensive amount of lovers before tying themselves down to marriage. For no woman wants a man who is a novice in the art of lovemaking.'

'And no woman wants a man who is so arrogant that he doesn't realise what a jerk he's being!'

'A jerk?' he ground out. 'You dare to call the sheikh of Zahrastan a jerk?'

'I do when it happens to be true.'

His eyes narrowed, but he could not deny the rush of blood to his groin, because her unprecedented insolence was inexplicably turning him on. 'And tell me this, Rosa Corretti—are you always so outspoken?'

In truth, no—she wasn't. The old Rosa was often button-lipped and uptight. She never voiced the scandalous thoughts which sometimes plagued her because that was the way she'd been brought up. To be serene and calm and ladylike. To hide her feelings behind a polished exterior. But what had been the point of playing her obedient role to perfection when everyone else had been deceiving her?

This man Kulal had deceived her too. He hadn't bothered telling her he was engaged to be married when he had practically glued himself to her on the dance floor, so why on earth would she tread carefully to spare his feelings? She doubted whether he had any!

'My outspokenness is irrelevant,' she snapped. 'And you haven't explained why you've made this astonishing proposal of marriage.'

'To protect my reputation,' he said.

She gave a short laugh. So he was self-serving as well as arrogant. 'Surprise, surprise.'

'And to protect yours.'

'I don't know what you're talking about.'

There was a pause while he chose his words, though he was finding it difficult to keep the irritation from his voice. 'My brother has found out that we spent the night together, so the information is out there. From what I understand, your own family is pretty good at information gathering.' He glanced at her from beneath the half-shuttered lids of his eyes as he watched her body tense. 'How do you think they might react if they discover you've been sleeping with an Arabian prince?'

She shuddered to think how they'd react if she'd been sleeping with anyone. 'But we didn't sleep together!' she hissed. 'You know we didn't.'

'And you think anyone is likely to believe that?'

Distractedly, Rosa rubbed the palm of her hand back and forth over her lips as his words hit home. With a shudder, she tried to imagine Alessandro and Santo's reaction to the news that their baby sister had been behaving like a *puttana*. The family would still be reeling from her mother's shocking disclosure—which would probably make their reaction even harsher than normal. She was still a Corretti, wasn't she? And a female Corretti, to boot. Bottom line was that her innocence would be seen as having been compromised, and all hell would be let loose. She could imagine them sending out a gang of heavies to bring her back again. Even worse—they might come and get her themselves.

'Mannaggia,' she whispered unthinkingly. 'What a fool I have been.'

It occurred to Kulal that not once during the entire conversation had she made any attempt to flirt with him, nor to show any kind of gratitude that he was offering a solution to her predicament. Why, she barely seemed aware of the bed in one corner of the room—a fact which was now beginning to dominate his thoughts. If it had been anyone else, he would have taken her into his arms and started to kiss her, but her face was so full of a simmering rage that he thought it unwise to try. He was beginning to realise that the situation was balanced on a knife edge, and that now he wanted her to agree to a plan which had initially repulsed him.

Because Kulal was an expert at finding the good in a bad situation. It was what had sustained him during his lonely childhood. He had refused to dwell on the fact that his mother's love had been brutally torn from him, and to focus instead on the unparalleled freedom which he had enjoyed within the palace walls. He had learnt to be utterly self-sufficient and hit out at anyone who should ever dare to pity him.

Now he looked at Rosa Corretti and thought about the benefits of having her as his wife. He thought about what enjoyment her curvaceous beauty would afford him. A body which he had touched only briefly would become his to play with as he pleased! And once his passion for her had worn off, he could send her on her way.

'A short marriage which can be dissolved once the dust has settled,' he elaborated. 'A marriage which could be beneficial to us both.'

She had lifted her head and was staring at him as if she was seeing him for the first time and didn't very much like what she saw.

'Beneficial?' she snorted. 'I think not. I think that marriage to you would be something of a nightmare.'

'Are you so sure?' he mocked.

'Absolutely positive!' she asserted, until she forced herself to confront an alternative which was even worse. She couldn't go home and yet she couldn't stay here with rapidly dwindling resources. Even if she ran to somewhere else and found herself a humble job, her family would surely come after her and find her. She forced herself to smile. 'But I can see that it would have some advantages.'

'You mean you're now agreeing to my proposition?'

'Only on certain conditions.'

'I'm afraid that won't be possible,' he stated softly. 'You don't get to bargain with a sheikh.'

'Oh, but I do!' she said firmly. 'Because you need this marriage more than I do!'

'You think so?'

'I know so.' She shot him a look of pure challenge. 'You're afraid of what my brothers might do when they find out about our liaison, aren't you?'

'Are you out of your mind?' His lips curled with derision. 'Kulal Al-Dimashqi is afraid of no one, Rosa. Not now and not ever. But I love my country and the fallout from our ill-advised night together could bring shame on our royal house.' There was a pause. 'You have no need to worry about tying yourself to me for a lifetime if that is what gives you cause for hesitation, for I will happily give you a divorce once a suitable time has elapsed.'

Rosa mulled over his words, aware that he was offering her a way out. It might not have been the way she would have chosen, but she wasn't exactly being dazzled by choice, was she? 'How long?' she questioned. 'Will we have to be married?'

He glimmered her a cool smile. 'How does a year sound?'

'Like eleven months too long?'

'I can assure you that it will fly by,' he said smoothly. 'Because time always does. Before you know it, the year will be up and I will send you on your way with a fortune big enough to guarantee your independence and a lifetime's memories of sexual bliss.'

Rosa met the gleam of his ebony eyes. His sexual boast was shocking and his arrogance was second to none, and yet... It seemed such a stupid thing to feel, but in the midst of all her confused emotions, she was aware only of a feeling of safety when she looked at him. Because whatever faults he possessed, she felt sure he would protect her. Nobody would dare come near her if Sheikh Kulal Al-Dimashqi was fighting in her corner.

Even if she could wave a magic wand—which is what she'd originally wanted—she knew now that her old life was over. She couldn't go back. She'd fled to France and booked into a cheap hotel and sold an old family bracelet and nearly got herself laid. For the first time in her life, she'd felt as if she was really living—the way her brothers were allowed to live—instead of existing in the pampered little bubble they'd created for her.

She'd tasted freedom and found it a heady brew and she could never return to the life she'd known before. All those eyes watching her. All those unspoken codes she'd grown up with, and the expectation which came with them. That Rosa was a good girl and that one day she'd marry some suitable Sicilian who had been picked for her.

If she was going to have to endure the ignominy of an arranged marriage, then why shouldn't she arrange it herself? Especially as this particular marriage had a get-out clause. She wanted independence and Kulal had offered it to her. He had offered her a generous pay-out too. For the first time in her life she would be independent! Imagine being able to do as she wanted, without having to run to someone else for permission. Her traditional family could not object once she'd got that all-important band of gold on her finger.

'It's a very tempting offer,' she said.

'I find it's always wise to make your offers tempting. It usually gets people to agree to them.' A smile slid across his lips as he slanted her a quizzical look. 'And your "conditions" are?'

Rosa hesitated. She had been about to tell him that it would have to be a celibate marriage. That she would not have sex with a man who thought so little of women—a man who had been prepared to cheat on his ex-fiancée without a flicker of conscience. But she could see now that such a demand would be impossible to enforce. Could she really imagine saying no to the sexual advances of a man like Kulal Al-Dimashqi? Could she really picture herself trying to resist him? She felt the sudden lurch of her heart.

Not in a million years.

She looked at the black eyes which glittered in his hawk-like face and in that moment she suspected he knew exactly what she was thinking. She could feel her skin tightening as their gazes clashed in recognition—as if her body was silently acknowledging the sizzling connection which blazed between them. She might not like what he stood for and she might disapprove of his views on women, but she wasn't stupid enough to deny that she wanted him.

The fact that he could treat his ex-fiancée so badly told her he wasn't a man to be trusted, but what man was? Even her own uncle had cold-bloodedly bedded her mother! She wasn't looking for trust, or softness—or any of the things which most women wanted when they took a husband. And with her family background, she certainly wasn't looking for love. Her mouth flattened. Definitely not love. She wanted someone to show her how to become a woman in the fullest sense of the word—and Kulal would be the ideal candidate. She would take from him everything he was prepared to give and then she would walk away.

'I've decided to waive my conditions,' she said, her airy tone matching the careless shrug of her shoulders.

Kulal saw the way her colour had heightened and again he smiled. 'I rather thought you might,' he murmured, his gaze drifting down to where her luscious breasts were jutting against the satin of her robe. He could see the nipples hardening as he watched them and he felt the responding jerk of desire. 'And that pleases me.'

'But I don't want my brothers finding out,' she continued. 'Because they'll try and put a stop to this wedding, if they do.'

For a moment he contemplated the idea of challenging her brothers—or laughing aloud at the very idea that their supremacy could challenge his. But why fight a battle which was ultimately pointless? They would get their precious Rosa back when the year was up. 'There are things we need to decide, but we can easily put them on hold.' His voice was husky as his gaze drifted once more to her nipples. 'And start occupying ourselves a little more pleasurably.'

She looked at him. 'Meaning?'

'You know very well what I mean, Rosa. Your body certainly gives every indication of doing so. And there's a bed right over there, just waiting.'

Rosa flinched as she crossed her arms over the betraying tightening of her breasts. 'Don't treat me like a whore, Kulal,' she said quietly. 'Or I'll walk away from this proposed union right now.'

He saw the way she had lifted her chin. Saw the glint of steel which had entered her dark eyes—and in that moment she looked very proud and very Sicilian. A formidable woman, he recognised as he inclined his head in a gesture of grudging acknowledgement. 'Very well,' he said softly. 'If such games amuse you, then we will obey convention and wait a little longer—and the anticipation will add spice to my growing hunger. I shall send a car for you in the morning. And in the meantime, you might want to give some thought to some appropriate attire.'

Her fingers touched the slippery silk lapel of her robe. 'What do you mean—appropriate?'

He wanted to say that stark naked would be his first choice and the skimpy crimson dress which had done such dangerous things to his blood pressure would be a close second. But not in public. In public she was going to have to play the part expected of her. They both were.

'Something which a future princess might wear on the way to meet her prince.'

She thought about the few clothes she had flung into her suitcase just before her impetuous flight from Sicily. 'I'll try.'

'And make sure you bring all your belongings with you.'

She looked at him warily. 'Why, where am I going?'

'To Paris.' He gave the ghost of a smile. 'To begin your new life.'

CHAPTER SIX

A NEW LIFE.

Kulal's words played repeatedly in Rosa's mind the following morning as she crammed down the lid of her suitcase. Was it possible to just shrug off your old life and emerge without any traces of it clinging to your skin? She snapped the suitcase closed. All she knew was that she was going to try—she was going to lose her troubled past and step out into a new and unknown future as the sheikh's bride.

Remembering Kulal's directive about appropriate attire, she chose a silk chiffon dress the colour of raspberry sorbet and black shoes which made her feel very tall—but she wore no jewellery, not even the ring her father had given her for her sixteenth birthday. Platinum bright and studded with emeralds, her hand felt strangely bare without it for she was never without it glittering on her little finger. But now it seemed to mock her and the relationship she'd enjoyed with her father. It made her question whether that, too, had been false, like everything else around her.

Had he known? she wondered. Had he realised before his own violent death that the daughter he'd so adored had been the child of the brother he detested? Had he been broken-hearted and careless as a result—dropping a match in that cavernous old warehouse which he and his brother had owned so that they had burned to death, their tortured cries carrying out on the hot, Sicilian breeze?

She was grateful for the loud knock which broke into her troubled thoughts and she opened the door to find Kulal's driver standing there. Wordlessly, he took her suitcase from her, leaving Rosa to follow him. But her questions about Kulal's whereabouts were met with a polite shrug. As if he didn't understand what she was saying—even when she spoke to him in French—and Rosa got the feeling that he understood her very well.

Her feeling of isolation grew as the car headed out towards the airport and she peered out of the window at the upmarket holidaymakers. Against the azure backdrop of the sea, there were women in tiny shorts, big sun hats and even bigger pairs of sunglasses as they hung around the harbour areas, as if waiting for an owner of one of the luxury yachts to pluck them up and sail them away to paradise. She thought how carefree they all looked as they fished around in their giant leather bags. As if they had nothing more taxing on their minds than when their next coat of lipstick needed to be applied. She wondered if they even noticed her—the woman in the expensive limousine being taken to marry a man who was little more than a stranger.

The powerful car slid to a halt at the Nice airport and she was escorted straight out onto one of the airstrips, where a large plane stood waiting on the tarmac.

Its gleaming jade-and-rose bodywork reminded her of some oversize exotic bird and a steward wearing matching livery ushered her on board. The light in the cabin was dim and it took a moment or two for her eyes to adjust to the sight of Kulal reclining on one of the seats, reading through what looked like a pile of official paperwork. He looked utterly relaxed, with his long legs stretched out in front of him and one arm pillowing his ebony head. Reluctantly, she ran her eyes over him in unwilling appraisal, unable to deny the sheer physical perfection of the man.

Did he hear her quiet intake of breath? Was that the reason for his enigmatic smile as his gaze flicked upwards?

'Don't look so frightened, Rosa,' he said softly, his eyes making their own leisurely journey down over the entire length of her body.

'I'm not frightened,' she answered, trying to convince herself it was true, even though that lazy scrutiny was making her skin tingle in a very distracting way. She told herself that she'd met enough powerful men in her twenty-three years to make her impervious to them. But she'd never met anyone who had looked at her quite like that before. He had removed his jacket and was wearing dark trousers and a white shirt with the sleeves rolled up. She could see the crisp sprinkling of hairs on his powerful forearms and, despite his relaxed pose, she was very aware of all the latent strength in his muscular body.

'Come over here and sit down,' he said, patting the elongated seat beside him.

She approached with the caution of someone walking towards an unexploded bomb, knowing it would sound naive if she complained that the angle of the seat made it look more like a bed. Yet a couple of days ago she'd wanted more than anything to find herself in bed with him. She wondered what had happened to that new and confident Rosa Corretti, who had looked at this man and decided that she wanted him.

Was it because this morning he was exuding a sex appeal which seemed intimidating and for the first time she realised that he was planning to deliver? That things had moved beyond the hypothetical and sex had become a reality. She was aware that his initial relaxed pose had gone and been replaced by a sudden tension—as if he, too, had suddenly acknowledged the close confinement of the aircraft cabin as the outer doors slammed shut.

She slid into the seat beside him, aware that he was still watching her, his dark eyes seeming to drink in every move she made. She told herself that she mustn't be intimidated. That she needed to be more like the woman who had pole danced her way into his line of vision, rather than the one whose heart was now beating out a thready tattoo. 'I hope that what I'm wearing is "appropriate,"' she said.

'Utterly.' He watched as she smoothed the delicate material of her dress over her bare knees. 'You will need an entirely new wardrobe to cope with the demands of life as a princess, of course—though I don't imagine you'll have much of a problem with that. I've yet to meet a woman who doesn't salivate at the thought of buying new clothes, especially when someone else is picking up the bill.'

Levelly, she met his gaze. 'Are you going to spend all your time denigrating women?'

'Not all my time, no.' His smile was edged with pure danger. 'I'm sure we'll be able to come up with something more exciting to fill our time.'

'Because...' She didn't want to let this go. She didn't want him to keep making comparisons—because wouldn't that just tap into her crippling certainty that she was going to disappoint him? That he had signed up for something and was going to get something completely different. 'I'm sure your knowledge of women is comprehensive—it's just a little off-putting if you're going to keep reminding me of the fact.'

'I'm sure your knowledge of men is equally comprehensive, Rosa.'

'You'd be surprised.'

'I doubt it. I've yet to meet a woman who surprises me.'

Rosa gave a little shake of her head. What a cynic he was. Shouldn't she have tried to hook up with someone softer—and kinder? Someone who wouldn't have whirled into her life like a very sexy tornado. The plane engines began to flare into life and suddenly she started to laugh—the unexpected sound taking her by surprise because it seemed a long time since she'd laughed at anything.

He raised his eyebrows. 'What's so funny?'

'Everything.' She looked at him. 'Within the space of a few short hours I've become the kind of person who steps onto a private jet with a man I don't really know—a man I'm going to marry. I'm going to be a princess and I'm going to live in Paris and I don't have a clue what my life will be like. It just doesn't…' Her voice trailed off as she met his eyes and shrugged. 'It just doesn't feel real, that's all.'

Once again, Kulal saw that fleeting look of vulnerability—the one which didn't match the sensual lips and hedonist's body. The one which was making his gut twist with an inexplicable unease. 'If it's any consolation, it feels pretty bizarre to me too,' he said flatly as the irony of the situation hit him—not for the first time.

He should have been contemplating matrimony with a high-born royal from a neighbouring country but instead he found himself with Rosa Corretti, the daughter of a nefarious Sicilian family with a terrifying reputation. One who flaunted her body like a hooker, but who had since denied him all but the briefest kiss.

His mouth twisted into a hard smile. He could feel the exquisite hardening of an erection beneath the fine cloth of his Italian trousers and he shifted his body a little. Why should he have to wait a second longer to enjoy all the sensual possibilities which her beautiful body offered?

From the galley, the steward appeared with a tray and Kulal said something terse in his own language, so that the man set the drinks down on the table and then quickly disappeared.

Rosa saw the way that Kulal's knuckles had suddenly clenched against the hard outline of his thighs. 'Is something wrong?' she asked.

'Something is very wrong.' Turning to her, he lifted his hand to touch her face, his finger slowly tracing the outline of her lips. 'You are driving me crazy, Rosa. I am aching to possess you and I cannot wait much longer.'

Rosa swallowed as he moved his hand downwards so that it was now lying directly over her breast and she wondered if he could feel the wild beat of her heart. His words were so…brazen. He made sex sound so straight-forward—as if doing it and wanting it was perfectly natural—but she had no idea how to answer him, because she had been brought up to think that it was wrong and forbidden.

'You are silent,' he observed, his fingers now drift-ing down over her belly before coming at last to rest on her knee. 'That is good. So often a woman destroys the mood of love with her inane chatter.'

Part of her wanted to scream at him for his arrogance, but no scream came—and how could it, when his hand had now drifted beneath the hem of her dress and she was holding her breath to see what he would do next?

His fingers began to slide upwards and Rosa's eyes closed as desire began to flicker over her skin—a desire which was powerful enough to obliterate any linger-ing feelings of guilt. He was drawing little circles just above her knee and, while it was exciting her, it was also frustrating the hell out of her. She began to wish that he would touch her somewhere else—touch her where she was beginning to ache like crazy. And maybe her restless little wriggle told him that, because his fingers had now crept up to reach the bare skin of her thigh. The warmth coiling somewhere deep inside her began to spread over her whole body and she could hear the loud thunder of her heart. Her thighs seemed to be parting without any conscious action on her part, and she expelled a breath of disbelieving pleasure as his fingers brushed intimately against the searing heat of her sex.

'Mmm,' was all he said.

'Kulal,' she breathed.

Waves of shock and excitement washed over her as he pushed aside the moist panel of her panties and began to move his finger against her aroused flesh and Rosa thought that nothing had ever felt this good. Nothing. She could hear strange, gasping little sounds echoing around the cabin, which she realised must be hers. She could feel the tension as her body strained towards something tantalising which seemed just out of reach. Something which surely promised more than it could ever deliver. And then it happened—almost without warning—like a shower of fireworks exploding unexpectedly in the sky. She found her body contracting with the most exquisite sensations, the force of them taking her by surprise. It felt like flying—and then afterwards it felt like floating down into some dreamy place, all boneless with the pleasure which was still washing over her. She gasped aloud as her head fell back. Her tongue snaked out to touch her mouth and even that made her sensitive lips tremble and for countless minutes she just lay there, drifting in and out of the most incredible daydreams.

'Unzip me,' he whispered.

His words broke into her dreamy thoughts and Rosa's lashes flew open to meet the opaque smoulder in his eyes. But there was no softness in them—nothing but hard-edged desire. Her gaze flickered to his groin and her nerve failed her.

'I can't,' she whispered.

'Why not?' He frowned. 'What's wrong?'

Rosa bit her lip and felt the sharp indentation of her teeth. A million things were wrong and, stupidly, the one which seemed to bother her most was the fact that he hadn't even kissed her. She realised that she had just had her first orgasm but Kulal had made it happen with all the cold-bloodedness of a scientist performing an experiment in a laboratory. She might want to learn all about sex but she hadn't intended her first real lesson to take place on an aircraft, and she certainly didn't want to be treated like some sort of faceless puppet.

She felt like someone who'd never skated before being put on an ice rink and told to dance. The other night when she'd been drinking, she'd been filled with an unfamiliar bravado as she had flung herself at him. Even the next morning, she'd still been disorientated enough to make an uninhibited pass at him. But now that the moment of truth had arrived, she was scared.

So why not tell him? Why not be upfront with him? Surely even someone as hard-hearted as Kulal might be gentle if he realised the true depth of her inexperience.

She drew in a deep breath and let the words out slowly. 'I'm a virgin.'

'Sure. And I'm Peter Pan,' he murmured, guiding her hand towards his groin.

'No,' she said weakly as she snatched her fingers away. 'I'm serious.'

He drew back from her and she couldn't quite make out the expression on his face. Surely that wasn't boredom she could read there?

'So am I, *habeebi*, so am I. So why don't we leave the role play until our appetites have grown a little more jaded? I know the fantasies which turn women on and we can do the "innocent virgin being ravished by the big, bad sheikh" to your heart's content, but for this first time, shall we just stick to what nature intended and adjourn to the bedroom?'

Rosa stared at him as his harsh words registered themselves in her befuddled brain. He didn't believe her! He didn't believe she'd never had sex with a man!

A wave of shame washed over her. Why should he believe her, after the way she'd behaved? He had signed up for a woman who shimmied around in a revealing dress, not an overprotected Sicilian girl who'd never felt the intimate caress of a man's hands on her body until now. And mightn't he be disappointed if he knew how naive she was?

Her mind began to race. This was supposed to be a marriage of convenience, for her convenience as much as his, but it wouldn't be very convenient for him if his new wife was a hopeless novice, would it? Maybe it would be better if he discovered the truth on their wedding night—when it was too late to turn around and tell her he'd changed his mind about marriage?

She tugged her dress back down.

'What do you think you're doing?' he demanded.

She met his incredulous look, trying to imagine what

a more experienced woman might say in such a situation. 'You're planning to have sex with me?'

'What do you think—that I want to discuss the state of the world's economy?' He glared at her. 'Of course I'm planning on having sex with you. Isn't that what you've been practically begging me to do since we first met?'

Rosa pursed her lips together, although she conceded that he did have a point. 'You want this to be our first time together?' she questioned. 'When any number of your crew could walk in and discover us?'

'I don't think so,' he snapped. 'My crew have strict instructions not to disturb me whenever I have a woman on board. No one will dare to come in.'

Rosa felt sick. Was he setting out to humiliate her, as she had seen men humiliate women so often before? 'You make a habit of having sex on this plane, do you?'

'No, Rosa, you're the first,' he drawled sarcastically. 'What do you think?'

'I think that as your fiancée, I should be shown a little respect.'

'Having sex with you doesn't show a lack of respect.'

She shook her head, because how could you shake off a lifetime's indoctrination in a couple of minutes? 'And what if I told you that it would make me feel cheap?'

He leaned back and surveyed her, one finger slowly tapping his lip. 'But acting cheap didn't particularly bother you when I made you come just a few minutes ago, did it?' He saw her blush with what looked like intense embarrassment but he did not heed it, his own intense frustration making him want to drive his argument home. 'Nor did you seem to feel cheap the other night, when you shamelessly flaunted your body at the club for all to see.'

She swallowed. 'I was drunk.'

'And do you make a habit of getting drunk? Is this something I should know?'

She met the accusation in his eyes and shook her head. 'No, I don't make a habit of it,' she said quietly. 'In fact, I've never been drunk before that night.'

His gaze grew thoughtful. 'So something led you to drink from the champagne bottle, like a workman slaking his thirst in the heat of the midday sun? Something which disturbed you enough to behave in a way which you say was uncharacteristic?'

His perception was appealing and Rosa wondered how much to tell him. She'd never been close enough to a man to even think about admitting what was on her mind before, though come to think of it, she hadn't known real intimacy with anyone. Her relationship with her mother had always been strained—and her two brothers would have run a mile if she'd started talking to them about feelings. They were Corretti men and they did that Corretti thing of buttoning up all their emotions—that was, if they even had any emotions.

Rosa had never known what it was like to speak from the heart, and as she looked into Kulal's cool black eyes she wondered if she could trust him enough to dare.

Yet what did she have to lose?

'I had just discovered something about my family,' she said.

Kulal forced himself to look interested in what she

was about to say, even if the last thing he was interested in was talking about her family. But he had learnt much about women during an extensive career spent seducing them, and had discovered that a little patience shown at the beginning paid dividends in the long run. He injected just the right amount of curiosity into his voice. 'And what might that have been?'

Rosa hesitated, knowing that she risked making her mother sound like some sort of slut if she told him the truth—and that women were inevitably compared to their mothers. But she had to remember that she wasn't trying to impress him. It didn't matter what he thought of her, not when her place in his life was so temporary.

Even so, she felt the painful twist of her heart as she said the words out loud and the bitter memories came flooding back. 'I discovered that my father was not really my father.'

Kulal shrugged. 'I imagine that must have been disturbing.'

'Yes, Kulal, it was disturbing,' she said drily.

'But you must realise that such a situation as yours is not terribly unusual. Don't they say that one in twenty-five children in the west are brought up by a man who is not their biological father?'

She blinked, because the last thing she had expected from him was a careless kind of acceptance. 'How strange that you should know something like that.'

'Not strange at all.' He shrugged. 'I happen to be something of an expert on these matters, since I've been the subject of several paternity claims.'

Her eyes opened wide and she felt the sudden anxious beat of her heart. 'You mean, you've got…children?'

He gave a short laugh, because she might as well have asked him if he had ever taken a trip to the moon. 'No, Rosa, I do not have any children—though one of the downsides to being a sheikh is that women have tried in the past to get themselves impregnated, in order to secure themselves a place in my life.'

Rosa stared at him in horrified fascination. He came out with the most outrageously chauvinistic statements—worse than her own brothers' at times—and yet somehow he managed to get away with it. Was that because his sophisticated exterior didn't necessarily reflect the true man underneath?

Because on the surface he might look like a modern playboy, with his sleek designer suit and his private jet, but beneath all the trappings he was nothing short of primitive. He was powerful and wealthy, yet he certainly wasn't predictable. His matter-of-fact response to her admission about her paternity had surprised her, and had removed some of the emotional sting from its tail—something she hadn't thought possible. And wasn't part of her grateful to him for that? Just as she was grateful for the almost effortless way he had just given her an orgasm.

Her cheeks grew pink as she remembered the way she'd let him touch her and the way that had made her feel. She couldn't carry on feeling daunted by his sexuality, could she? Despite what she suspected was a very selfish nature, he had just proved to be the most generous of lovers. And surely she should be generous back.

How difficult could it be to give a man pleasure? Why not get it over with, so that it was out of the way and that she wouldn't have to dread it any more?

She lifted her hand to his face, letting her fingers slide over his sensual mouth, and even that brief touch felt electric. As she let her hand drift to the unopened neck of his silk shirt, she could see the suspicion which narrowed his eyes and her words of explanation came out in a breathy rush. 'Maybe I've changed my mind,' she whispered. 'Maybe we could make love after all—if you say that your staff would be sure to leave us alone.'

There was a split-second pause. A moment when she saw anger and frustration darken his face, before he swiftly removed her hand from his neck.

'You think you can play with me, as a cat would a mouse?' he demanded. 'That I am a man who can be picked up and put down? Are you nothing more than a tease, Rosa?'

'No!' she protested. 'I never meant to tease you. I was nervous, that's all—but I think I'm over that now.'

'Well, that's too bad,' he responded acidly, shifting his aching body away from her. Maybe it was time he showed her who she was dealing with—that he was not the kind of man to tolerate a spoiled little girl's sexual games. His smile was cold. 'It's not going to happen. At least, not right now. The flight to Paris only takes fifty minutes and I'm afraid we've wasted most of them talking.'

Rosa felt her heart clench. Wasted them? When she'd opened up to him like she'd never done to anyone else? When she'd let him touch her body as nobody had ever touched it before. When she'd decided that maybe she could trust him enough to tell him the truth about her parentage, only now it seemed that he was throwing it all back in her face. When would she ever learn that the only person she could really trust was herself?

'How silly of me,' she said lightly.

'Very silly,' he agreed, though the tremble of her lips made him briefly wonder whether it was worth telling the pilot to circle the plane so that he could indeed seduce her. Wouldn't ridding himself of this terrible ache make such an indulgent breach worthwhile?

And yet, hadn't he been partially responsible for this very unsatisfactory turn of events? He had been leaning forward, about to kiss her, when he had been arrested by the look on her face as he had touched her so intimately. He had never seen a reaction so instant nor so rapturous and hadn't he just watched her with a kind of dazed voyeurism, instead of undressing her and starting to make love to her?

He shifted his body as he decided against a delayed landing. Maybe it was better this way. The fantasies he had been building about his feisty little Sicilian should be enjoyed in slow time—not in some rushed explosion of need in the rather limited confines of an aircraft.

He snapped shut his seat belt and subjected her to a cool stare. 'In life, I find that timing is everything. Maybe that's something you should bear in mind for the future, Rosa.'

CHAPTER SEVEN

KULAL'S BREATH CAUGHT in his throat as Rosa entered the Damask reception room of the Zahrastanian Embassy, looking like a vision in her bridal finery. He stared at her, finding it hard to reconcile the pole-dancing temptress with the woman walking slowly towards him. By necessity, the white gown she wore was modest, covering her entire body so that only her hands and her neck were left bare. Her dark hair was coiled on top of her head and the lace-trimmed veil was held in place by a priceless diamond-and-ruby tiara from the Al-Dimashqi collection.

Inexplicably, he felt the sudden twist of his heart, for she looked… His gaze drifted over her and he gave a small shake of his head. She looked beautiful. More beautiful than any woman he'd ever seen and he wondered if his senses were inevitably heightened by the significance of the ceremony which was about to take place.

They had been apart ever since his car had dropped her off at the Plaza Athénée Hotel yesterday, after a tense and silent journey from the airport. He had spent the night alone at his own apartment, simmering with a sexual frustration which was completely new to him. Naked, he had tossed and turned in his vast bed while the events of that bizarre flight to Paris had taunted him. Rosa had refused to have sex with him, and had then inexplicably changed her mind, just before coming in to land. He had never met such a capricious woman before!

The wedding had been scheduled—without fanfare—to take place within hours of their arriving in the French capital because he didn't want the world's press to get wind of it. Inevitably, word would get out sooner or later and then the palace's slick PR machine could whirr into action. But someone must have talked—the way they always did—which had meant that he'd been forced to clear a path through the waiting photographers who'd been standing outside the embassy when he had arrived earlier.

But now his bride was here and any lingering misgivings he might have been harbouring were dissolved by that tentative look she was slanting at him from behind the misty cover of her veil. How well she played the part, he thought approvingly. That faux shyness was remarkably convincing and he knew that the embassy officials would approve of her demure appearance.

'Rosa,' he said as he stepped forward and raised her hand to his lips.

Rosa could feel his warm breath on her fingertips and the tantalising promise of his touch only added to her general feeling of disorientation. Even discounting the fact that she was standing in an exquisite bridal gown in the middle of the Zahrastanian Embassy, the man she had agreed to marry now looked like a stranger.

Today, his playboy reputation and urbane appearance were nothing but distant memories. The immaculately cut suit had been replaced by a flowing garment of white silk and his hair was covered with a headdress of the same colour, held in place by an intricately knotted band of golden thread. He looked dark and indomitable, and the starkness of his robes seemed to emphasise the chiselled contours of his face.

Rosa swallowed down a feeling of nerves. 'The place is swarming with press,' she said.

Kulal shrugged. 'Weddings are news, I'm afraid.'

'Particularly a wedding involving a sheikh who was recently engaged to someone else and particularly if he's marrying a woman from a notorious family,' she answered drily. Rosa stared down at the sparkle of her brand-new ruby-and-diamond ring, which had been hastily despatched to her hotel by motorcycle courier late last night. She supposed there might have been less romantic ways for a man to give a woman an engagement ring, but right now she couldn't think of one. She looked up into his face and once again she couldn't help herself from being stirred by his proud, dark beauty. 'I can't imagine how my family are going to react when they find out what I've done.'

'They're going to have to accept it because they'll have no choice. And you'll no longer have to fear their influence, Rosa, since from now on you will come under my protection.'

Protection. It was a word which meant different things to different people, but it had particular resonance for someone from Sicily and Rosa gave him an ironic smile. 'One cage exchanged for another, you mean?' she questioned lightly, glancing up at the high, moulded ceilings of the exquisite embassy room. 'Even if this cage is considerably more gilded than the one I knew at home.'

'You seem to forget that this marriage is nothing but a temporary arrangement,' he said softly. 'One which has been manufactured to satisfy our critics. It's not as if it's going to be a lifetime commitment.'

Kulal's words nagged at her conscience throughout the short service which followed and Rosa thought about the woman he'd previously been engaged to. Had she heard about this wedding and was she lying and sobbing her heart out on some faraway pillow, thinking about the man who got away?

And then, rather more selfishly, Rosa thought about herself, knowing that she was here on false pretences, in more ways than one. She held out her hand so that Kulal could slip on the glittering diamond wedding band, knowing that he'd be expecting great things from her in the bedroom and she wondered how he was going to react when he discovered the truth. What was he going to say when he discovered that the only thing she knew about sex was that amazing orgasm she'd had on the plane?

'You may now kiss the bride,' said the celebrant.

Rosa stared up into the gleam of Kulal's eyes and held her breath as she waited, but the swift, almost perfunctory graze of his mouth over hers left her feeling oddly rejected.

Her disappointment was so great that she summoned

up the courage to rise up on tiptoe to put her lips close
to his ear. 'That wasn't much of a kiss.'

'I agree that it was briefer than any kiss I have ever
given any woman, but I fear that once I start kissing you,
I may not be able to stop.' He linked his fingers in hers
and gave them a squeeze, putting his lips to her ear so
that nobody else could hear. 'And perhaps it would be
inappropriate for me to ruck up that pretty dress and
take you unceremoniously against the wall, which is
what I feel like doing.'

'Kulal!' The word trembled from her lips. 'That's the
kind of thing a savage would say!'

'But perhaps my "savage" words turn you on, my
beauty.' His black eyes gleamed with challenge as he
observed the sudden flush of colour in her cheeks. 'Am
I right?'

And although she shook her head to halt his erotic
line of questioning, the truth was that he was turning her
on. Turning her on in a way she wouldn't have thought
possible, especially when all he was doing was holding
her hand. Rosa could feel her breasts pushing against the
bodice of her gown, as if they were anxious to be freed
from their lacy confinement. Her mouth was drying and
her skin was tightening with anticipation, so that she felt
almost dizzy. But even though she felt a little daunted
by this rush of unfamiliar sensations, she met his eyes
with a sudden fearlessness, recognising that this was her
opportunity, her time to grow. She had married Kulal
to be free and independent, not to cower in the corner
just because he was making her body respond to him
in a way which was perfectly natural.

'Yes,' she said softly. 'Your words turn me on. They turn me on very much, if you must know.'

She saw the sudden tension which passed over his face before he nodded. 'Then let's get this next bit over with,' he said, sliding his arm around her waist. 'Let's go outside and give the press exactly what they want.'

But despite his warning, Rosa was unprepared for the wall of blinding light as the embassy doors were opened onto the street, where the small number of photographers had grown into a jostling crowd.

'Rosa!' someone yelled as the flashlights flared. 'What do your family think about you marrying a sheikh?'

'Rosa, how do you think Kulal's ex-fiancée is feeling today?'

Rosa could feel herself stiffen, but Kulal pressed his fingers into the flesh at her waist.

'Smile,' he instructed softly. 'Look like you're having fun.'

But she felt almost paralysed by the flashbulbs and the damning nature of the questions and maybe Kulal realised that, for suddenly he turned her towards him, his lips parting so that she could see the gleam of his teeth.

'Seems like I'm going to have to kiss you properly after all,' he said.

'And is that such a hardship?' she whispered.

'Everything about me is hard at the moment,' he commented drily as he lowered his mouth onto hers.

For a moment, the only thing Rosa was aware of was the press going crazy, but then the outside world blurred and faded and she was aware of nothing, other than the sensation of his lips exploring hers. Desire raced through her, as if he'd turned on some powerful current. As if she was on fire. She pressed the palms of her hands against his chest, revelling in the feel of his powerful torso, until she realised that he was pulling away from her and that the kiss had come to an abrupt end.

His eyes were impossible to read as he stared down into her upturned face, as if he was seeing something there which he had not expected to see. 'That's the first time I've ever kissed a woman in public and I don't think it's an experiment which needs repeating. I think I'd better get you back to my apartment as quickly as possible,' he said, his mouth barely moving for fear that some clever lip-reader in the press corps could pick up on what he was saying. 'Before we're hauled up on a charge of public indecency.'

Rosa could feel herself blushing as his bodyguards began to clear a way through the press, but she was surprised when Kulal waved a dismissive hand at the driver, who was opening the door of his official car. 'No. We'll walk,' he said. 'It isn't far.'

'But, Highness—'

'I said we'll walk.' And with that, he took her hand in his and began to lead her along the street, his mood unexpectedly buoyant as they began to walk along the wide boulevard. He stared down at their interlocked fingers, suddenly aware of the fact that he'd never held hands with a woman in public before. Her skin was the delicious honeyed shade which denoted her Sicilian upbringing, but his own was very much darker and there seemed to be a certain erotic association about the contrast between the differing hues. 'And smile,' he added softly.

It was the most bizarre experience of Rosa's life, walking in her lace wedding dress through the exclusive streets of the sixteenth *arrondissement*, her new husband beside her in his flowing white robes. Bodyguards speaking furiously into earpieces shadowed them all the way and people stopped what they were doing to turn and stare. She saw cars slowing down and drivers leaning out of their windows to capture their image on cellphones, and there were yet more press waiting outside his upmarket apartment block. She wondered if there would have been quite so much fuss if Kulal hadn't been wearing his traditional robes—and that only added to her sense of unreality. As if he was some kind of fantasy figure, rather than an ordinary man. But he isn't an ordinary man, she reminded herself, and this whole marriage was the stuff of fantasy.

He gripped her hand tightly as yet more flashbulbs exploded in her face, but this time she felt much less intimidated. She waved away the question of what her family would think or how her brothers would respond. Sustained exposure to something meant that you could get used to it and Rosa found she was even able to smile at one of the more persistent lens men. She felt breathless with nerves and a growing excitement as they walked into the foyer and took the elevator up to the penthouse suite, with Kulal watching her in speculative silence all the while, as if he didn't quite trust himself to speak. She kept telling herself that she wasn't going to be scared by what was about to happen. She had wanted adventure, hadn't she? Well, she had certainly found it!

Still silent, he opened the door to his apartment and Rosa stepped into a huge entrance hall. She had been prepared for luxury and she wasn't disappointed. Impressionist paintings adorned the walls and she'd never seen so much antique furniture outside of a museum. On dark, wooden floors lay faded silk rugs which looked centuries old and she wondered how many different pairs of feet had walked over them. She thought that a place like this could never really feel like home—or more specifically her home, until she remembered that it was never intended to be.

She found herself trained in the spotlight of his dark eyes as he watched her, like a hunter silently following the progress of its quarry.

'Drink?' he questioned.

'Just…some water would be fine.'

He led her into an incongruously modern kitchen of steel and granite and poured her a glass of ice water which she drank standing up, still in her wedding dress. She noticed that he didn't drink anything himself, and when she'd put her empty glass down, it was to find him still watching her.

'I want you in my bed,' he said simply.

She held her breath for a long moment before she expelled it. 'Then take me there.'

She could sense the growing tension in his body as he led her through a maze of corridors straight into the biggest bedroom she had ever seen, where vases of crimson roses stood on every available surface, their powerful perfume scenting the air. Tall windows overlooked a perfect vista of Paris, where the Seine was glittering in the afternoon sunlight, and beyond that she could see the arching fretwork of the Eiffel Tower.

'As you see,' he said. 'I have made every preparation for our honeymoon. I have even arranged for the sun to shine.'

Rosa glanced around the room, thinking that it looked gorgeous, but slightly unreal—as if a magazine shoot was about to take place. A vast four-poster bed played host to banks of pillows and shiny cushions and a bottle of champagne stood in an ice bucket on a small table nearby. And now there was nothing to stop them. No curious air crew or officials or intrusive cameras hovering nearby. Now she could give herself up to what she had been aching to experience for so long. She was going to start living the way other people lived, and for the first time in her life she was going to have sex.

She saw that he was staring at her and the pounding in her heart increased.

'Do you know, I have never seen a woman look more beautiful,' he said, swallowing down an inexplicable lump in his throat and finding himself surprised by his reaction. Was that because she had resisted him? Because she had not let him have her on the plane? He had never waited so long to have sex with a woman and the postponement of pleasure was making him ache. With a commanding finger, he beckoned to her. 'Come here.'

The look in his eyes was so irresistible and the yearning inside her so strong that Rosa went straight into his arms.

'I think it's time that I undressed you,' he said unsteadily. 'Don't you?'

'Yes,' she answered, with shy assent.

First he removed the ruby-and-diamond tiara and put it down on a nearby table and then he unclipped her veil with dextrous fingers and let it slither to the ground.

She closed her eyes as he lowered his head to kiss her and she honestly thought she might pass out with the sheer pleasure of that kiss. She was aware of the powerful scent of the roses and the way his hands were moving over her body, caressing her curves as if he was determined to explore every inch of her. She scarcely noticed him sliding down the long zip of her dress until it had pooled in a circle of lace around her ankles and she was left standing in nothing but her underwear. The cool air rushed onto her skin as he dragged his mouth away to study her and she should have felt nervous, but the expression in his gaze was making her feel anything but nervous. This felt right, she thought exultantly. Like what she had been created for.

'You look…' But Kulal's voice trailed off because, once again, the sight of her had taken his breath away. Her breasts were spilling out of a low-cut white bra and the matching high-cut panties were digging slightly into the soft curve of her hips. He'd never seen a woman who looked so fleshy before and it took a moment before he could compose himself enough to speak again. 'Exquisite,' he finished raggedly. 'The most beautiful thing I have ever seen.'

Rosa reached her hand up to touch his face, his words filling her with confidence as she reminded herself of the woman he had been attracted to—the one who had danced so provocatively on that podium. She had not been shy. So she began to tug at the white silken headdress as if undressing a man was something she did every day of the week. 'Why are you wearing this?' she asked as she removed the whole contraption, including the woven golden headband. 'I've only ever seen you in a suit before.'

He took the headdress from her and threw it on top of the tiara. 'Because usually I prefer to blend in. I find that people are much more accommodating when they think you're just like them.'

'But you're not?'

He laughed. 'Of course I'm not. I am like few other men—for how can I be? I was born in a palace and reared as a son of the desert. People always see me as a playboy and I can act that role to perfection. But in my heart I am a sheikh.' There was a pause as he looked at her. 'And for once I wanted to look like one.'

'Why?'

There was a pause as Kulal considered her question but the truth was he didn't know what had motivated him to reach for his thawb this morning, instead of a sleek designer suit. He frowned as he forced himself to remember that this was all for show. That the symbolism of the ceremony meant nothing. 'For the press, of course.' He traced his finger over the centre of her cushioned lips. 'It will make a great picture in tomorrow's papers.'

Rosa nodded but she could feel a sinking sensation of disappointment. So he had been playing up for the cameras all along. Was that the reason for the kiss on the steps of the embassy, the one which had felt so electric—because it provided a great photo opportunity, rather than because he'd been longing to kiss her as she had him?

But this was what she had signed up for, wasn't it? An expedient marriage which they could both walk away from.

'It will make a fantastic picture,' she agreed, stepping out of the discarded dress and staring up at him, her heart now beating very fast. She was just going to have to forget about her feelings and be the woman he thought she was. That woman would have listened to nothing but the desire which was rising up inside her, making her want to rip off his silken robe and feel his skin beneath her fingertips. And maybe he'd read her mind, for he kicked off his shoes before suddenly peeling the garment from his body in one swift movement, and Rosa gasped when she realised that he was completely naked underneath.

Kulal smiled, for her gasp pleased him—though it was certainly not the first time he had been greeted with such a reaction when a woman saw his body for the first time. He reached down to touch the hard ridge of his erection as he met her startled eyes and gave a lazy smile. 'Worth waiting for?'

Rosa swallowed down a mixture of excitement and fear because she'd never actually seen a naked man before, but she mustn't beat herself up about it. She reminded herself that generations of women had started their wedding night in a similar state of ignorance. It might be old-fashioned, but it certainly wasn't a crime.

'Definitely,' she said truthfully, and it was obviously the right thing to say, for he gave a satisfied nod before picking her up in his arms and carrying her over to the bed.

She felt the soft mattress dip beneath their combined weight, and as he lowered his head to kiss her, she was aware of his practised fingers removing her underclothes until she was as naked as he was. He kissed her with a passion which left her breathless—as if he was making up for lost time, and under the sweet and relentless torment of his tongue, Rosa moaned with pleasure.

His hand was on her breast, his fingers tiptoeing their way down over her belly, and suddenly her own hands were exploring him and it felt like the most natural thing in the world. She revelled in the hard planes and muscular lines of his body, which were so different to the fleshy contours of her own. She thought about what had happened on the plane and she wasn't sure how fast these things were supposed to move, but they seemed to be happening very fast indeed. For a moment Kulal pulled away from her to tear open a little foil packet which was lying on top of a cabinet next to the bed—and maybe he saw her confusion because in the midst of stroking it on, he gave a satisfied smile.

'I told you that I had everything prepared for our honeymoon.'

He moved over her and she could feel the wetness between her thighs and the slight resistance as he started to push inside her. For a moment he stilled and she prayed that he wasn't going to stop, so she sank her lips against his shoulder and grazed at his skin with her teeth. And the simple gesture seemed to flick a switch somewhere deep inside him as, with a low growl, he began to move.

It wasn't anything like how she'd thought it would be. She hadn't realised that it would feel so...intimate. That the joining of their flesh would make her feel so incredibly close to him. She was pliant in his arms, content to let him lead and to learn from him, so that when he lifted up her thighs she wrapped them around his back. And when his hands slid beneath her buttocks to pull her even closer, she gasped aloud at the sensation of his deeper penetration.

She knew what an orgasm felt like, but the one she experienced now was magnified by the sensation of Kulal deep inside her body and his mouth exploring hers in the most sensual of kisses, his fingers tangling luxuriously in her hair. Sensation ripped through her like a forest fire as every pore of her body seemed alive with a blissful kind of awareness. She felt her back arching helplessly beneath him and dug her nails into his back as the incredible spasms ripped through her. It took a while before she opened her eyes to find him watching her, black eyes narrowed with every sweet thrust he made. And then those eyes became wild and hectic, his movements increasing before he made a guttural cry and slowly came to a shuddering rest on top of her.

For a while she felt dizzy and overcome by the most delicious wave of torpor. Her fingers crept up to his shoulders and began lazily to knead at the flesh there. She wished that she could capture that moment and bottle it, knowing that if she could it would sustain her for the rest of her life.

'You were a virgin,' he said at last, breaking the silence.

'Yes.' A pause. She prayed that would be enough because she didn't want to break this delectable mood, but his dark eyes were hard and questioning and, reluctantly, she shrugged. 'I told you that on the plane.'

Kulal rolled away from the cushioned curves of her body and shook his head. He remembered the first time he'd ever had sex, at the age of sixteen—and afterwards the palace maid had given him a hand-rolled cigarette. He remembered the way the rough tobacco had scorched its way down into his lungs and he had never smoked since, but now he found himself wishing that he could inhale some of that sickly sweet smoke and make himself dizzy.

'I didn't believe you,' he said slowly. 'You certainly didn't act like an innocent.'

'Blame the drink.'

'And what else do I blame, Rosa? Or should that be "who"?' He lifted her chin with his finger and the green and gold flecks in the depths of her eyes looked bright and vivid. He saw the uncertainty which flickered across her face, that strange vulnerability which appeared when you least expected it, and he shook his head in disbelief. 'You're twenty-three years old and you've never had sex with a man before today?'

'I thought we'd just established that.'

'I'm asking why.'

'And do you always subject your lovers to questioning, straight after...' She thought about how best to phrase it. She knew that people called it 'making love,' but there'd been no love involved in what had just happened, had there? 'Straight after having sex with them?' she finished baldly.

'Up until now, no. But then up until today I've never had a virgin—or a wife, come to that.'

'Bit of a double whammy?' she questioned flippantly.

'You can wisecrack until the sun comes up, but I'm not going to be satisfied until you've answered a few of my questions.'

Rosa wriggled uncomfortably, because she didn't want to think about it. She didn't want to think about anything. All she wanted was to hang on to this delicious warmth which was still pulsing through her body. She wanted to cling on to the amazing memory of what had just happened until it happened again, but she could see from the hard glint in his eyes that he had no intention of letting her avoid his questions. Why was he so damned persistent? she thought.

'I lived a very restrictive life in Sicily,' she explained. 'It's not unusual there, even these days, for a female to be wrapped in cotton wool until she is married. I was the only girl and I had two fiercely overprotective brothers, except that they...'

Rosa's words trailed off and Kulal heard the sudden bitterness which had crept into her voice. 'They what?'

Rosa pursed her lips together, her first instinct to come up with some fabrication about her past, but what was the point of telling lies? If she shocked him with the ultimate truth, then maybe the marriage would be even shorter than either of them had intended. Except that suddenly she realised she didn't want it to be. She felt as if they'd only just started on their own particular journey and she wanted more of it. Even if it wasn't real, she wanted more of that stuff which felt like intimacy.

'They're not my brothers. I've just discovered that they're actually my…half-brothers.'

He frowned. 'I don't understand.'

How could he possibly understand when she was still having difficulty grasping the facts herself? So that now she would be forced to say out loud the words which still made her want to retch. 'That's why I ran away from Sicily,' she said, and drew in a ragged breath. 'Because I found out something which rocked my whole world.'

'Go on,' he said.

She stared at him, wishing more than anything else that what she was about to tell him wasn't true. But it was. True and horrible and irreversible. She swallowed. 'There was a huge family gathering—a wedding which never happened—and my mother got drunk. Very drunk. I could hear her shouting, even above the sound of the music, but I couldn't quite make out what was being said. And when I did, well—' She swallowed down the bitterness which had taken up residence in her throat. 'I couldn't believe it.'

She remembered her mother's face looking flushed and contorted. She remembered the sudden lull in the music as Carmela's slurred words had echoed around the room. Awful, shocking words which had chilled her to the bone. They still did. Rosa tried to stop her lips from trembling as she stared into Kulal's face, but it seemed that this was something else which was beyond her control. She took another deep breath. 'I discovered that my father was not my father,' she said.

'You already told me that on the plane.'

'I discovered that my father was in fact my uncle,' she finished painfully, just so that there could be no misunderstanding. 'My mother slept with my uncle.'

She was unprepared for the violence of his reaction. She saw his face darken as if some kind of violent storm was brewing there. She sensed that he was about to move away from her even before he actually did. He unpeeled himself from her warm body and got off the bed, walking to the other side of the vast room where he stood there surveying her, as if she was an alien species who had just dropped into his life from another world.

CHAPTER EIGHT

SHIVERING FROM HIS sudden departure from the bed and from the new coldness in his eyes, Rosa met Kulal's accusing gaze.

'Your mother slept with your uncle?' he demanded in a voice which was icy with disbelief.

'Yes.' She tried not to flinch, thinking that it sounded even worse when it came from someone else's lips. And Kulal clearly thought so too, because his face had frozen into a sombre mask. 'But this is terrible!' he flared. 'I have rarely heard anything more shocking.'

'You think I don't know that?' she questioned. 'You think I wouldn't give everything I owned for it not to be so?'

'Is this not incest?' he questioned, almost as if he was speaking to himself.

'No! No!' And to Rosa's horror, she burst into tears. All the tears she'd been bottling up ever since her mother had blurted out the horrible truth now came spilling out. She hadn't dared to give in to the danger of crying before, terrified that once she started she might never stop. She had needed all her energy and her strength to get away from Sicily and the dark web of deceit which had been woven into her life for all these years. But now that the tears had begun, they seemed unstoppable. They slid down her cheeks and onto her breasts, dripping from the prominent curves to fall in a growing damp mark on the pristine linen sheet. 'I d-don't know what it is, but it's not that,' she declared raggedly. 'My mother and my uncle were not related by blood.'

'But they were related by honour!'

'Yes, they were!' She glared at him, wiping away the falling tears with a clenched fist. 'Don't you think this has been difficult enough, without you, a complete stranger, getting on your high horse and taking the moral high ground?'

'But I am not a "complete stranger," Rosa. I am your husband!'

His words seemed to bring her to her senses and she shook her head. 'But only as a symbol,' she whispered. 'As an expedient measure which suits us both. You're not a real husband, Kulal—and a marriage of convenience doesn't give you the right to stand in judgement of me, especially when this was something which was completely out of my control.'

For a moment there was a silence. Kulal stared at the fierce set of her lips, as if she was determined not to cry again. And he saw something in her which he recognised with a painful twist of his heart. Something he had buried so deep that he had almost forgotten its existence but which was now reflected in Rosa's tearstained eyes. It was powerlessness, yes, but it was anger too—that in a single moment, your life could change for ever. For him, it had happened when his mother had scrambled up a rock to go to the aid of her trapped child. For Rosa it had happened when her mother had looked at her husband's brother with lust in her eyes.

Damn the past, he thought viciously. And damn the never-ending repercussions of that past.

He walked across the room towards her and sat down on the edge of the bed, watching her gaze slide briefly to the roughness of his naked thighs before she turned her head to stare into his face instead. He could see the wariness which had frozen her features and he took one of her cold hands in his. 'You should have told me all this before,' he said.

'And would you have still married me?'

There was a pause as he imagined the reaction of the press, if ever this were to get out. He could read the desperate question in her eyes and he knew it would be the easiest thing in the world to tell her what she wanted to hear. But wasn't it about time that people stopped lying to Rosa Corretti?

'I don't know,' he said heavily.

It was not the answer she wanted, but strangely enough it comforted her. Much better to hear the harsh truth than honeyed words which meant nothing. And this was an honest relationship, wasn't it? That's what it had been from the very beginning. They hadn't pretended to feel things they didn't feel and they didn't need to say things they didn't mean. 'You think it's an easy thing to tell someone something like that?' she questioned. 'That I'm not burning up with shame having to admit it to you now?'

He heard the guilt which had distorted her voice and

once again he felt the simmer of anger. 'Of course it's not easy. But this is not your shame. You are nothing but a victim in all this, Rosa.'

'And I don't want to be a victim! I'm fed up with being a damned victim!' she declared, shaking her head so that her dark hair flew wildly about her bare shoulders. 'But what would someone like you know about that?'

He heard the resentment in her voice and usually he would have brushed away her question, with all its inquisitive undertones. He didn't tell women things about his feelings or his past because there was no need to. He kept his secrets hidden from everyone, even from himself. But her admission had made him feel uncomfortable—more than that, it had ignited painful memories which had lain dormant inside his own heart for so long. What could you say to a woman like Rosa Corretti, who had been forced to face such an intolerable situation? Wouldn't it only be human kindness to open the door on his own suffering?

'I know more than you would ever guess,' he said slowly. 'And at least you can rest assured that the dark secret in your life and the consequences of that secret were outside your control. At least you are not responsible for what happened to you.'

She could hear the terrible pain which laced his words and saw the way that his face had frozen into a forbidding mask. The hard gleam in his eyes was piercing through her—as if daring her to ask him more—and she suspected that a look like that might put most people off. But Rosa did dare, because what did she have left to lose? 'What happened?'

Kulal shook his head, but that did nothing to keep the memories at bay. He remembered a story that his English tutor used to tell him. The story of a man called Orpheus, who had been told never to look back. But Orpheus had looked back and had been left broken-hearted as a result. Kulal had never forgotten the moral of that story—that looking back could destroy you, and going forward was the only way that you could survive. 'It doesn't matter,' he said bitterly.

'Oh, but I think it does,' said Rosa softly. 'And I think you want to tell me.'

He turned on her then, his face dark with the deepest sorrow Rosa had ever seen, and she held her breath as she waited.

'I caused the death of my mother,' he said bitterly.

For a moment she didn't speak. She wanted to brush away the bald statement like unwanted dust, but the suffering she saw on his face warned her not to make light of it. 'How?'

Kulal glowered. He had been expecting her to respond with a placatory 'Of course you didn't!' because that was what everyone always said, even if their accusatory eyes carried an entirely different message. 'You want to hear how?' he demanded. 'Then I'll tell you.'

Rosa leaned back against the pillows and shiny cushions and nodded. 'Go on, then.'

There was something so unexpectedly calm about her that Kulal did something he'd never done before. He completely disregarded the fact that she was naked and that her cushioned breasts were just crying out to have him lay his head on them. Instead he opened his mouth and let out the words which had been smouldering away inside him for so long that they seemed to taint the air with their darkness. 'I was six years old,' he said. 'And a very naughty child, apparently.'

She nodded. 'Most six-year-old boys are naughty.'

'I don't need you to try and reassure me, Rosa!'

'I was merely pointing out a fact.'

'Well, don't!'

She shrugged. The fury in his voice would have been off-putting to a lot of people, but she had grown up with furious men whose word was law and she knew how to deal with it. She lay very still and watched him.

Kulal picked his next words carefully; he felt like someone plunging his hand into a basket of fruit, knowing that angry wasps were buzzing inside. 'It had been a hot summer, piteously hot—with the worst drought our country had ever known. Sandstorms had been raging in the desert for weeks and we had all been confined to the palace. We were going stir-crazy. I remember feeling that so vividly. I remember the constant drip of sweat, despite the fans that whirred overhead. My older brother was away in Europe, and I missed his company. But my mother said we would go on a picnic as soon as the weather improved and one morning the storm just died down, as if it had never happened. There was a strange calm to the air—and even though my mother complained of a slight headache, I was eager to leave.'

He was silent for a moment. How eccentric the memory could be, he thought. How was it that something which you'd blocked for over thirty years could suddenly reappear in your mind, as crystal clear as if it had happened the day before? Were these things he remembered himself, or things he had been told? Or maybe they were just a combination of things he had pieced together after the event.

'We were driven out to Saxrasahl—a very famous dried-out plain which was once an oasis and is surrounded by intricate rock formations.'

Rosa nodded. She wanted to say that it sounded beautiful, but this was something she could never say, for his voice was leaden with the sound of approaching doom and she knew he would never associate such a place with beauty.

'We ate our food, but I was eager to play and there was nobody to play with. My mother's headache had grown worse and the driver and the bodyguards were too hot to join in with me. My mother told me to stay within eyeshot, but I remember being engrossed in my game. I remember climbing to the top of a rock, but the dryness of the terrain meant that it started to crumble. I...screamed.' He closed his eyes and his heart began to pound. 'And I heard my mother's voice calling my name—and soon after that, I saw her face appear, for she had climbed the rock to find me.'

He stared down at his hands, as if he might find some comfort in those tight, clenched fists. The silence seemed to go on and on until Rosa reached out and touched one shoulder which was so hard and unyielding that he might as well have been carved from stone.

'And then?'

He lifted his head and it was as much as she could do not to recoil from the heartbreak written in his eyes. 'Her foot slipped. The bodyguard yelled—for he was only feet away from her—but it was too late. She fell.'

She forced herself to ask the painful question, because what else could she have said in the circumstances? 'And she died?'

He shook his head. 'Not straightaway. She was airlifted to hospital but she never came out of the coma. She slipped away two nights later, with my father holding her hand.' A father who had never really forgiven him and a brother who had returned from Europe to accuse him of putting their beloved mother in danger. Later, both men had done their best to try to make up for the words which they'd uttered in the depths of their own grief, but it had been too late. And no blame or accusation had ever been more condemnatory than that which Kulal had directed at himself.

As his voice died away, Rosa stared at him, wondering what on earth she could say to a tortured man who had just bared his soul. What words could possibly bring him comfort? She thought about everything he had missed—all the cuddles and the warmth and knowing that somebody who loved you more than anyone else in the world would always be there for you. And then she felt a sharp and bitter pang of understanding, because she'd never had a mother like that, had she? She moved closer, her arms slipping around his neck as she offered him all the comfort in her heart.

'I'm sorry,' she whispered. 'So very sorry.'

He tried not to flinch but the warmth of her body

was irresistible. He had told her more than he'd ever told anyone. His playboy mask had slipped and she had glimpsed the real and ravaged face behind. He felt raw and he felt vulnerable. He felt all the things he had vowed never to feel again.

'It doesn't matter,' he said unevenly.

'Of course it matters.' She saw the bleakness etched onto his features as she dared to bring up the one glaring omission from his story. 'When your mother died, did you never think that perhaps her headaches might have been contributory? Was a post-mortem ever done?'

'No!' Her questions only added an extra layer of pain to his bitter memories and, pulling away from her, he steeled himself against her look of concern. Did she think that he was regularly going to bare his heart to her and subject himself to this kind of pain? And if that was the case, then surely it was his duty to enlighten her.

'That's it, Rosa,' he said flatly. 'We've had this conversation because maybe it was necessary, but we won't be having it again. We've looked inside our individual wardrobes and seen all the skeletons hanging there, but now we're closing the door on them. Do you understand?'

She heard the finality in his voice. 'If that's what you want.'

His eyes narrowed. 'Yes, it's what I want, but maybe it's not what you want. Because this wasn't what you signed up for, is it?'

'I don't think either of us really knew what we were signing up for.'

'Which is why I'm giving you the opportunity to walk away.'

'Walk away?' Rosa blinked at him. 'What are you talking about?'

'Leave. Go on. Leave now. Why not? It makes perfect sense. You'll still get your pay-off—only you'll get it sooner than you ever anticipated. Because I think I've done rather better out of this marriage deal than you.' He forced himself to say the words—wanting her to hate him, because if she hated him, then she would go. She would go and he wouldn't have to look into her eyes and realise that she knew his secret and that she had seen his pain. 'Just think, Rosa—all that money I'm prepared to pay for having taken your virginity. You can walk away now—free and independent, just like you wanted.'

But Rosa didn't move because she knew exactly what he was doing. He was regretting having confided in her and now he was trying to drive her away. He was offering her money and trying to make her sound like some kind of whore in the process—something she'd emphatically told him she would not tolerate. Hoping that she'd leave here in some kind of rage.

A few hours ago and she might have been tempted, but that had been before he'd taken her to his bed. Before he'd shown her what she was capable of feeling. There was a reason it was called sexual awakening, she realised. Something had happened to her, and it was all down to him. It felt as if she'd been existing in a shadowy place before Kulal had brought her senses to life. And she didn't want to lose this feeling.

'Going is the last thing I want,' she said, and knew she hadn't imagined the long breath which escaped from his lips.

'Then what do you want?'

She took the edge of the linen sheet and began to pleat it between her fingers, because that was easier than looking into those piercing black eyes. She recognised that she wasn't ready to go it alone—at least, not yet. Not when the world outside Sicily still seemed such a big and frightening place. Wasn't the whole point of this bizarre marriage that Kulal could give her something which nobody else could? Not just the money which was going to buy her independence, but a sexual education which had only just begun. And why should anything be allowed to spoil the best thing that had ever happened to her?

Looking up, she pushed the heavy fall of hair back from her face and the movement caused her heavy breasts to sway. She saw him shift a little and her attention was caught by the growing erection between his thighs and in that moment she felt shy and powerful, all at the same time. 'I want you to teach me everything you know.'

He stared at her, knowing that he should distance himself from her and yet how could he when she looked so damned gorgeous? How could he force her to leave when he wanted her so much that he felt he could explode with need? He could smell the lingering scent of sex on the air and could feel the erratic beat of his heart as he leaned forward and bent his lips to her neck. 'Anything specific you have in mind?' he questioned unevenly. 'The history of Zahrastan, maybe? Or the new energy proposals I'm setting out next week?'

She tipped her head back. 'About pleasure,' she whispered through dry lips. 'Teach me everything you know about pleasure. I'll be your wife and one day I will walk out of your life. But in the meantime...'

'What?

She wriggled again, more impatiently this time. 'Please?'

He drew back to see the sudden rush of colour to her cheeks and something made him want to show her who was in charge. To show her that, ultimately, he was the one who called all the shots. And perhaps the first lesson she needed to learn was how to articulate her own desires, instead of expecting him to second-guess them. Because only that way would she ever be truly independent. 'Please, what?' he prompted softly.

Rosa met the dark gleam of his eyes, and swallowed. 'Please will you do it to me again?'

CHAPTER NINE

KULAL STROKED HIS fingertips over the silken curtain of dark hair which lay spread all over the pillow and felt the inevitable hardening of his body.

'I know you're awake, Rosa,' he said softly. 'So why don't you open your eyes and kiss me?'

Rosa stirred as the sheikh's voice penetrated her dreamy thoughts and, obediently, she let her eyelashes flutter open. He was lying next to her, propped up on one elbow—deliciously naked and gloriously virile, studying her body as if it was the most beautiful body he'd ever seen, which was what he had told her in the early hours of this morning as he had pulled her hungrily into his arms. Each morning she woke up to a similarly appreciative reaction, but it still took some getting used to.

She pushed the blanket of mussed hair away from her face and yawned. 'But I might have been asleep,' she objected.

He glanced at his wristwatch. 'It's nearly midday.'

'And it's Saturday. Or are you saying that it's impossible for someone to be asleep if it's nearly lunchtime?'

'I knew you weren't asleep because you've been

wriggling that delicious bottom—' he smiled as his arm snaked around her waist and he turned her around, so that his erection was pressing hard against her belly '—against me for the past half-hour. So it was a toss between going for a cold shower, or seeing if I might be able to get you to do something more interesting than sleeping.'

She leaned forward, brushing her mouth against his and feeling the instant shimmer of lust which flamed over her skin. 'You can always get me to do that,' she said, her voice sounding almost shy as he cupped her buttocks to pull her closer. But wasn't it insane to feel shy, when in the few short weeks since their marriage Kulal had stripped her bare in just about every way there was?

He had taught her so much. He had shown her that sex was something to be enjoyed and savoured, not something furtive and shameful. In short, he had liberated her from a lot of her own hang-ups and all she was trying to do now was avoid getting too dependent on a man who was never intended to be anything other than a temporary fixture. 'In fact, you can get me to do just about anything,' she finished softly, and saw his eyes darken.

'I know,' he said. 'And I'd be happy with pretty much anything you'd care to do to me right now.'

'Oh, Kulal.'

'Oh, Rosa,' he murmured back, and lowered his head to kiss her. He thought that her lips felt cool and tasted of the peppermint tea she'd brought back to bed when they'd first woken. Her arms tightened around him and the desire he felt grew stronger—his heart beating out a crazy rhythm as he pushed one hard thigh against the fleshy softness of hers. He thought how perfect she was in his arms, how their lovemaking just got better and better and pretty much took his breath away every time. And he thought how their honeymoon had surprised him in all kinds of ways.

At first, they had barely left the apartment—with only the occasional trip to a theatre or a restaurant punctuating their lazy days and long nights of sexual exploration. For the first time in his life he had cleared his diary and turned off his phone—because he never took a holiday. Never. He told himself that it would be a useful experiment to see if his charitable foundation could function well without him, but deep down he knew that wasn't the real reason. The truth was that he didn't want to leave Rosa's side. He couldn't get enough of her; he couldn't seem to keep his hands off her. And when they had ventured out, he had felt like a tourist in his adopted city. She'd made him do things he would normally never have dreamt of doing, like climbing as far as it was possible up the Eiffel Tower—with his bodyguards trailing behind them. And when he had remonstrated that he did not wish to join in with other sightseers, she had halted his objections simply by kissing him.

'You're never too cool to see the whole of Paris from the top of the Eiffel Tower,' she'd giggled against his lips. And later that week they had taken a riverboat down the Seine and she had looked up the name of all the bridges in her guidebook and recited them to him. They'd sat and drunk coffee incognito at the famous

Café de Flore and made two similarly unrecorded trips to the theatre. In fact, they'd managed to avoid a single press photographer capturing any honeymoon images and to Kulal this had felt like a small triumph—especially when he'd realised that she actually hadn't been interested in being photographed with him.

He'd even taken her shopping—something he'd never done before, although he'd picked up plenty of inflated bills in his time. But with Rosa it was different. She didn't seem bothered about the cost of things and he enjoyed dressing his new wife with clothes which befitted a princess. Just as he enjoyed buying—and removing—the outrageous scraps of silken underwear which could barely contain her luscious curves.

He still couldn't get his head around it. What was the appeal of lying next to her and just watching her—as if the sight of the slow inhalation and exhalation of her breath was the single most fascinating spectacle in the world? Usually he absented himself pretty early, because he didn't like women hanging around him in the morning. He liked his space and his privacy. He liked the feeling of being alone—the way he'd always been.

But not with Rosa—and he was still trying to work out why.

Was it because she gave herself to him so completely? Because she was all his and only his—like a newly minted coin which had been held by no other person? With her, he felt primeval. Something possessive and powerful gripped him whenever he held her, something which battered at his senses like a raging storm. Perhaps that was the ancient power of the marriage vows—that no matter how carelessly the words had been spoken, they still managed to convey a profound significance to the couple involved.

He moved his head down between her thighs, hearing her breathless little gasp of anticipation as he began to lick her. He revelled in the taste of her sweet-sharp stickiness and the way that his fingers sank into her soft hips—just as he revelled in her orgasm as she bucked helplessly beneath his tongue. He stayed there for a while, his lips pressed hard against her until at last she grew still and then he moved over her, and into her. He closed his eyes as he lost himself in her slick heat. Allowed the urgent rhythm to spiral them both up to a place so high that the slow and incredible fall back to earth left him breathless, and spent.

He must have fallen asleep, because when he opened his eyes it was to the smell of strong coffee and the sight of Rosa sitting on the window seat in a silken robe the colour of claret, with the glory of Paris framing her like an Impressionist painting.

'I've made you some coffee,' she said.

'I can smell it.' He sat up as she placed it on the table beside the bed. 'You make the best coffee in the world.'

'This is true,' she said seriously. 'Because I'm Sicilian and we do the best of everything.' But as Rosa lifted the pot to pour her own coffee, she was aware of how hollow her words sounded. She used to revel in her Sicilian roots and identity, with the fierce pride which had been drummed into her ever since she could remember. Being born and raised on the beautiful Mediterranean island had always given her a feeling of belonging. She'd felt part of her family and also part of the bigger island community, which had always existed there. But not any more. Her mother's betrayal seemed to have had even wider-reaching repercussions than she'd originally anticipated. Not only had her relationships within the family been dramatically altered, but a wall of silence seemed to have descended since Rosa's dramatic flight from her homeland.

'Have you heard anything from your family?' he questioned softly.

Had he read her thoughts, or had her wistfulness shown on her face? She didn't want to show him she was hurt because she was trying very hard not to be. But it did hurt that neither of her brothers had been in touch, even though she'd emailed them her new phone number and told them she was now married and living in Paris.

'I've heard from Lia,' she said slowly. 'She's the half-sister I never knew I had. The one I insulted after my mother had dropped her bombshell. I wrote and apologised for the way I lashed out at her and she was so sweet. She said she understood. She also said she'd always wanted a sister—she just hadn't been expecting to find one quite so dramatically! But I guess we'll never get to know each other now.'

Kulal frowned. 'There's nothing stopping you going back to Sicily, you know—if you wanted to speak to them face to face,' he said. 'I could take you there, if it would help.'

Rosa shook her head. And have everyone cluster round and want to find out about her glamorous new husband? She wasn't that good an actress and somehow she couldn't bear the pity she'd have to endure when her family discovered the truth of why they'd married. 'I told you—I can't imagine me ever wanting to go back. There's no place for me there now. The person I used to be doesn't exist any more.'

Because the new Rosa was now a princess, even if it was only a very temporary role. She didn't get to wear a crown but she got to share the bed of a man who was a real-life prince. A desert sheikh—a man who couldn't seem to get enough of her…and much as she revelled in his attention, she knew it was getting dangerous. She'd been feeling that for days now. It happened every time she opened her eyes and saw him lying next to her and it continued throughout the day. She hugged the memory of their lovemaking to her like a delicious present. She'd never felt so contented—nor ecstatic—in her whole life and she knew that it would be madness to allow her feelings for Kulal to grow.

But how did you stop yourself feeling something when your heart was determined to do the opposite? She picked up her cup and sipped her coffee. She could not afford to get too attached to her husband, because one day they were going to split. She knew that. She'd signed that damned pre-nup, hadn't she? The one which offered her a massively generous amount of money, in exchange for a 'clean break' settlement? She just needed to train herself to get used to that bald fact and to maintain some kind of emotional distance.

She tried telling herself she was okay with it, when Kulal announced that their honeymoon was over and that he was planning to return to work at his foundation the following Monday. But the reality was that she'd wanted to cling to him and beg him not to go and that feeling had scared her more than her very real dilemma—about how to usefully spend her days while he was working.

'I'm not sure what I'm going to do all day in Paris, with you back at the office full-time,' she said.

He glittered her a smile. 'Do more of what you did in Sicily. You were a lady of leisure there, weren't you?'

Rosa didn't let her smile slip, even though it wasn't the most flattering way to describe her former life. It was true she hadn't had a career, though she'd been awarded a respectable languages degree from the University of Palermo. But it had been difficult to find a job which hadn't been vetoed by her controlling family. She'd done bits of interpreting work whenever she could, but opportunities were scarce. So she'd ended up with a part-time administrative job at the university where she'd studied—and it had felt a bit like stepping back in time. As if she hadn't progressed much beyond the student she'd once been.

'I wasn't exactly a lady of leisure,' she defended. 'I did have a part-time job—'

'Well, there's no need for you to have a part-time job now,' he said, a touch impatiently. 'Just enjoy your days and let me pick up the bill.'

Rosa tried not to feel offended by his dismissive words just as she tried to throw herself into her new life as a stay-at-home Parisian wife. She explored more of Paris and the many attractions it had to offer. She walked everywhere—always tailed by the ubiquitous bodyguard—and began to gain the confidence which came from learning the geography of a once-strange city. In the mornings she took in a gallery or an exhibition, and in the afternoons she went to see a film and her once-fluent French began to improve as a consequence.

But she got a distinct sense that she was simply filling in time, that she was becoming like many of the other rich expatriates who counted away their hours with culture. She began to look forward to Kulal's homecoming with more enthusiasm than she told herself was wise. He didn't want an eager woman throwing herself at him like an underexercised puppy whenever he came home from work, did he? He wanted a woman who'd had an interesting day, because surely that way she'd be more interesting herself.

One evening, he came back late from the office and went straight into the shower, and when he walked into the bedroom, Rosa was sitting in front of the dressing table in her bra and pants, blow drying her hair.

'You haven't forgotten we're out to dinner tonight?' he questioned, momentarily distracted by the sight of the lace-covered globes of her breasts.

'No, of course I haven't.' She put the hairdryer down and watched his reflection as he began to rub a towel over his damp body. 'We're seeing someone from a TV company, am I right?'

'You are. Actually, the executive producer of one of France's most successful independent companies, who wants to make a documentary about Zahrastan.'

She met his eyes in the mirror. 'Maybe that's a good thing—to place it in the minds of the public.' She leaned forward and slicked some lipstick over her mouth. 'I'd never heard of Zahrastan until I met you.'

'Precisely.' Roughly, he rubbed at his hair. 'We need to let the world see that we're not some big, bad oppressive dictatorship. The biggest problem was persuading my brother to allow a foreign crew to enter the country in order to film.'

'And he was agreeable?'

Kulal laughed. 'Oddly enough, he was very agreeable—since he's notoriously prickly about foreign opinion. But I think he's decided that Zahrastan has to be seen as embracing the modern world.'

'And do you...' She hesitated, because since that first night, when he'd poured out the blame and guilt he'd felt about his mother's death, he'd barely mentioned his brother. In fact, the frankness of that night had not been repeated, even though she had tentatively tried to get him to open up on more than one occasion. But he had blocked her moves with the skill of a seasoned chess player. She got the feeling that he had allowed her to see a rare chink in his armour and had no intention of repeating it and it frustrated the hell out of her. Because wasn't it natural to want to chip away at that armour and see more of the real man beneath? Didn't that kind of intimacy feel just as profound—maybe even more profound—as anything which they shared during sex? She sucked in a breath as she watched him pull on a white shirt. 'Do you talk to your brother much?'

He raised his eyebrows, as if she had somehow overstepped the mark. 'Obviously we've spoken about the film crew. How else would I know his feelings on the subject?'

The faint sarcasm which edged his words was new but Rosa wasn't going to give up, because this was the first opportunity she'd had in ages. 'I don't mean about that. I mean, about…about what happened to your mother.'

She saw him stiffen before his eyes suddenly became cool and watchful. Like a snake's eyes, she found herself thinking as a little flutter of trepidation whispered over her skin.

'Sorry?'

'I just thought—'

'Well, don't,' he snapped. 'Because there's nothing left to say on the subject, Rosa. I thought we'd already decided that.'

His words were steely—they sounded like a metal door being slammed—but Rosa wasn't going to give up. She knew the danger of locking away painful things. You locked them away and they festered and then one day they all came bubbling out in a horrible mess. Wasn't that what her own mother had done? 'I just get the feeling that there's so much between you which isn't resolved. That maybe—'

'Maybe nothing,' he clipped out, and now his words were coated with ice. 'I told you those things because…' Kulal felt a brief flicker of anger, but it was directed at himself as much as at her. What the hell had possessed him to tell her all those things? To open up his heart in a way which was unheard of? 'Because you'd given me a brief glimpse into your own sorry family saga and I decided it was only fair to try to redress the balance. But I didn't tell you so that you could suddenly decide to "fix me."' He stared at her. 'You have enough things to worry you, Rosa—and if you feel the need for some sort of redemptive programme in your life, then I suggest you might try working on your own stuff first.'

His attack had come out of nowhere and it startled her. Rosa stared into his hawk-like face and thought that his expression looked cruel and almost…unrecognisable. Except that wasn't strictly true, was it? He had looked at her that way when she'd woken up in his villa. When she'd found herself alone in his bed and discovered him staring at her as if he didn't like her very much.…

She fished around for something to say. Something which wouldn't involve bursting into tears and demanding to know why he'd felt the need to spoil everything with his cruel words. But instead, she fixed him with a questioning look which was very polite and utterly shallow. 'What kind of documentary?'

He nodded, as if approving her sudden change of subject. 'A groundbreaking one, with not a camel in sight.'

She gave the smile she knew was expected of her before walking into her dressing room to choose something to wear. Her hands were shaking as she pulled open the closet door, but she tried to tell herself that she couldn't heap all the blame on Kulal.

Because in a way he was right, wasn't he? She hadn't worked out any of her own stuff. She still felt bitter and hurt by what she had learnt about her parentage. She had run away from her family, but it seemed that her family had been happy to let her go—and she was surprised by the sharp pain she felt as a result. Had she thought she was still their precious Rosa who could do no wrong? That they'd come seeking some kind of reconciliation or to comfort her, when the reality was that they would have been furious and humiliated by her desertion?

She began to riffle her way through her clothes, picking out an ankle-length dress, which Kulal had chosen for her himself. It was a simple red dress, but the beauty was in the fabric which clung like molten syrup to her curves. Skyscraper heels in ebony leather and loose hair completed the look, though impulsively she clipped a scarlet silk flower behind her ear at the last minute.

Kulal's reaction to her appearance was gratifying, although she had to reapply her lipstick after he'd kissed it all away, and still glowing from the sweetness of that kiss, she decided that she was going to forget the bitter words he'd spoken. What was the point of ruining the evening ahead, especially when he looked so…gorgeous. His dark, sculpted features were highlighted by the fact that he was newly shaved and his ebony hair gleamed in the early-evening sunshine as they stepped into the official car.

Was it normal to feel this way? she wondered. To want to touch him at every given moment and run her fingers over each inch of his body? But she didn't give in to her desire—just sat serenely beside him on the back seat of the large car, asking him intelligent questions about the proposed documentary, so that by the time they arrived in the trendy Marais area of the city she felt composed. As if she had been born to walk into swish restaurants by the side of a man who had caught the attention of every person in the room.

The TV executive was called Arnaud Bertrand, and if she'd been with anyone other than Kulal, Rosa might have found him attractive. His chiselled jaw and sensual mouth hinted at his earlier career as an underwear model, before he'd realised that it was far better to rely on his brains, rather than his beauty. Or so he told Rosa, during a lull in the conversation, when Kulal was busy talking to the location manager about the practicalities of taking a film crew to Zahrastan.

'Whilst you,' he mused, his eyes moving to the bright flower she wore in her hair, 'could rely on both, I think. Brains and beauty.'

'I'm not beautiful,' she said quickly.

'You don't think so?' Arnaud narrowed his eyes. 'With that lustrous hair and perfect skin, you remind me of Monica Bellucci. And you are the wife of one of the world's most powerful men, a man who could have any woman he chooses. That in itself speaks volumes about you.'

Rosa bit back a wry smile. If only he knew why Kulal had ended up with this too-curvy Sicilian with a complicated past! 'And I'm certainly no academic,' she said, swiftly changing the subject and wondering if he paid such lavish compliments to every woman who entered his radar.

'But you're a linguist, right? You speak French and English—and Italian, of course.'

Rosa shrugged. 'Plenty of people do.'

'But plenty of people do not look like you, Rosa.

You have a freshness about you—and a vibrancy too.' Arnaud lifted his wine glass to his lips, and over his shoulder Rosa thought she could see a faint frown appearing on Kulal's brow. 'Tell me, would you be interested in taking a screen test?'

Rosa blinked. 'You mean for television?'

'Of course for television—that's my medium.'

'I don't act,' said Rosa bluntly. 'And don't they say that the camera adds ten pounds? I'm completely the wrong shape for the small screen—I'd fill it!'

'Ah, but I believe in smashing stereotypes,' said Arnaud softly. 'I'm trained to recognise that certain *je ne sais quoi* which the camera loves and I think you have it. I'm not expecting you to act, just do a brief test. Would you be interested?'

Telling herself that it would be rude to refuse his offer—or maybe that it would simply be easier to go along with it—Rosa took his card and slipped it into her handbag.

'Ring me,' he said, and then turned back to talk to Kulal.

The dinner was delicious and the wines kept on coming and Rosa felt wonderfully replete as their car arrived to take them home. But even though she made a few predictable comments about how well the evening had gone, Kulal merely answered her in clipped monosyllables. His powerful body seemed tense and forbidding, but she was feeling expansive—and more than a little bit randy—so she trickled her fingertips over his forearm. But he didn't react and, feeling foolish, she quickly removed her hand as if it had been contaminated. He didn't say another word until they were back at the apartment and the lights which bounced nightly off the Eiffel Tower were flickering over the huge sitting room, making it seem as if they were standing in the centre of a silent fireworks display.

'You seemed to hit it off very well with Arnaud,' he said slowly.

'That was the whole point, surely?' She clicked on one of the lamps, telling herself she was imagining the scowl of accusation on his face. 'I was there as your wife, to support you—and the best way I could do that was to be friendly.'

His black eyes bored into her. 'Did being friendly involve thrusting your breasts in the face of the executive producer?'

Rosa tensed as she heard an ugly and unmistakable note in his voice. It was a note she knew too well from having grown up in a family of powerful men. Men who had an overabundance of male testosterone and an overinflated sense of their own importance. It was possession—pure and simple—and it made her skin turn to ice.

She tried to keep the tremble of outrage from her voice. 'That's a completely unreasonable thing to say.'

'You think so? Then why did he give you his card? You think I didn't notice that?'

The card was buried at the bottom of her handbag and Rosa honestly didn't think she would have given it another thought if Kulal hadn't challenged her, but his attitude was riling her. More than riling her—it was making rebellion stir up inside her. Because hadn't she fled Sicily precisely to avoid this kind of domineering attitude? To stop people treating her as if she was some puppet whose strings they could pull at will.

'He asked me if I was interested in taking a screen test.'

'You?'

'Yes, me, Kulal—is that such a bizarre thing for him to have said?' she demanded, pushing aside the nagging voice which reminded her that he was only echoing her own initial reaction.

'And you told him no?'

She heard the certainty in his voice and drew in a breath as her emotions began to wage a sudden and dramatic war. She knew what he wanted and she knew she could please him by telling him exactly what he wanted to hear—but then what? You caved into a bully once and that was giving him carte blanche to bully you all over again. She had planned to do nothing about Arnaud's offer of a screen test, but now she was beginning to have second thoughts. She stared at her husband, not liking the Kulal she was seeing tonight, knowing that he had no right to dictate what she should or shouldn't do. Because surely he hadn't forgotten that this marriage wasn't real?

'I haven't told him anything,' she said. 'At least, not yet.'

There was a pause as Kulal stared at her. 'But you're going to tell him that you're not interested,' he said.

Rosa's mouth dried as she felt the sudden tension in the room. Because that had been a statement, not a question. Or rather, it had bordered on being an order.

Rebellion flared up inside her once more. 'I'm going to hear what he has to say,' she answered stubbornly.

Kulal could feel a tight knot of anger but he could feel something else too. A flicker of something which burned beneath the anger and which was growing like a weed inside him. Something painful and intolerable. Something unfamiliar and yet horribly recognisable. He rammed his hands deep into the pockets of his trousers—something he couldn't remember doing since he'd been a schoolboy and had been sent to that terrible prep school in England. But he didn't want her to see the bunched tension of his knotted fists. Because wouldn't that reveal the fact that he was in pain—and he didn't want to be in pain!

He gave a tight shrug of his shoulders. 'Suit yourself,' he said coolly. 'I'm going to bed.'

Rosa watched him go. He'd sounded so dismissive, as if he didn't want her to share his bed that night. She licked her lips. So was she going to let herself be intimidated? Crawl off to sleep in one of the empty bedrooms as if she'd done something wrong, when all she'd done was to consider a perfectly reasonable offer which had been made to her.

Like hell she was!

She went to the bathroom and stripped off her dress, then brushed her hair and washed her face—and when she had removed every trace of the evening, she heard something behind her and glanced into the mirror.

Not something.

Someone.

Kulal stood behind her—completely naked and completely aroused by the look of him. On his face burned an expression she'd never seen there before. Was it anger or desire, she wondered, or a potent mixture of both? She saw the heat in his black eyes and instinct was telling her that maybe sleeping in one of the spare rooms was a better idea than slipping into the marital bed when he was in this kind of mood. Anything would be better than having to face that undiluted rage on Kulal's face.

But that was before he put his arms around her. Before he dropped his lips to her shoulder and traced a line there—the words he uttered made indistinct by his kiss. But they were not tender words. They were words of want, not words of need. They were graphic words about what he wanted to do to her, and although the baldness of his erotic wish list made her feel that she should beg for sleep and ask him to wait until morning, Rosa did no such thing.

His hands were far too clever to let her escape. His fingers made her weak with longing and so did his lips, so that by the time he entered her from behind, she was as turned on as he was. Turned on enough to watch their dual reflections in the mirror when he urged her to do so. Turned on by the sight of her own orgasm—and just as turned on by the sight of his.

But even though the kiss he gave her afterwards was lazy and sticky, he disentangled himself sooner than she wanted him to. She wanted him to stroke her and comfort her; to tell her to forget about the hurtful things he'd said. But he didn't. The only thing he told her was that he needed to do some work before he slept.

And he didn't follow her to bed.

CHAPTER TEN

ROSA AWOKE TO an empty space beside her and when she blinked open her heavy eyelids it was to see Kulal pulling on a jacket. He was dressed for the office in dark trousers and a pristine white shirt and she shifted a little to get a better look at him, but she noticed that he made no acknowledgement as she stirred.

She sat up in bed, a chill creeping over her skin as she remembered the angry words of the previous evening which had culminated in that cold, almost anatomical sex in the bathroom. She shivered. At the time it had turned her on like mad to see the wild passion flaring in their eyes, as they'd watched their reflected images bucking their way to fulfilment with all the guilty pleasure of voyeurs. But now it all seemed curiously empty. Vividly, she recalled those big, dark hands cupping her breasts and the look of fierce intensity which had shadowed his face as he'd thrust into her. It was like watching a rerun of a porn show and felt like the emotional equivalent of a hangover and her cheeks began to burn with shame. How could she have let herself do that, when in the previous few moments he had been damning her with his snide accusations about flaunting her body? Accusations which hadn't even been true.

Which left the question of how she was going to handle the situation this morning. Did she bring up the whole painful subject and risk one of those dreadful circular arguments which went nowhere? Or should she just be grown up about what had happened? Forget what had been said the night before and start the new day on a new and positive note.

She sat up in bed. 'Morning!' she said cheerfully.

He turned round then and Rosa could see the shuttering of his dark eyes.

'I didn't want to wake you,' he said.

Suddenly, she felt self-conscious. He was dressed in that immaculate suit, while beneath the sheet she felt naked and vulnerable. She wondered if he, too, was remembering last night's erotic scene in the bathroom, and some unknown instinct made her pull the sheet a little higher. 'I didn't realise you were going to work so early.'

He shrugged. 'There are things I need to do.'

The smile she attempted was more difficult than she'd thought—especially when he was talking to her in that polite, cool tone, as if she was someone he'd just met at a party. No, maybe not at a party—because then he would be smiling back at her. He wouldn't be looking at her with that flat expression in his eyes. 'Surely as the boss, you can be excluded a crack-of-dawn start!' she said, her voice just a little too bright.

'It's not a question of being excused, Rosa—more that I have plenty of ongoing projects which need my attention.' Kulal buttoned his jacket, acknowledging how false her words sounded. And suddenly he realised that the honeymoon was over; it had ended last night when those dark feelings had taken him to a place he hadn't wanted to go. When he'd looked at her and experienced a blinding jealousy at the way she'd flirted with the Frenchman throughout dinner. He remembered the painful pounding of his heart as he'd stared into an abyss which had seemed uncomfortably familiar—and it had taken all his energy to regain his usual clarity of mind.

He wondered if she was feeling more reasonable today. If she'd woken up and realised that Arnaud Bertrand had simply been using her as a means to try to get closer to him. He surveyed her curvaceous body which was outlined by the white sheet. 'So what are you planning to do today?'

For a moment she hesitated, because she knew the most acceptable way to answer his question. She could fake a light excitement about visiting some art gallery or exhibition, or recount the synopsis of a film she was intending to see.

But Kulal's behaviour last night had scared her. It had shown her the ruthlessness he was capable of. It had painted a dark picture of what he could be like if things didn't go his way, and it had served as a timely warning that she needed to protect herself. She needed to guard against her own stupid emotions—the ones which had started tricking her into thinking that Kulal had started to care for her. Because he hadn't. She didn't have a special place in his heart just because the sexual chemistry between them was so hot.

It was important to remember something else too—

something she hadn't dared admit until now. That if she let herself start to care for him, then she would get hurt. Badly hurt. She'd go back to being a victim—the kind of woman who things happened to, instead of making them happen for herself. And he wasn't exactly falling over himself this morning to tell her that he had spoken impulsively and out of turn, was he? He wasn't apologising for all those insults he'd thrown at her last night.

She remembered the way she'd capitulated to her controlling family for all those years and she twisted a strand of hair around her finger. 'I thought I'd give Arnaud a ring.'

'Arnaud Bertrand?'

'He's the only Arnaud I know.'

He could feel the rapid flare of rage, but somehow he kept his expression neutral. 'I thought you'd decided that wasn't a good idea?'

'I don't remember saying that.'

'Maybe not in so many words.' His eyes narrowed as he tried not to dwell on the area of her breasts which was not concealed by the sheet. 'But in the cold light of morning, perhaps you've considered the general unsuitability of a sheikh's wife flaunting herself on television.'

'I wasn't planning to do anything to bring your name into disrepute, Kulal.'

'No pole dancing, then?'

'That's unfair.'

'You think so? You wish to deny the past, perhaps?'

She met the accusation in his eyes and she wanted to tell him to stop doing this. To stop it right now before he did irreparable harm to what they had. She wanted to rewind the clock back to yesterday morning, when his words had been tender, not harsh. 'You know why I pole danced,' she said quietly. 'I was drunk and I was running away from an impossible situation. You know that.'

His black eyes continued to bore into her. 'So what are you running away from this time, Rosa?'

She could feel the hammering of her heart as she clutched at the sheet. 'I'm not running from anything,' she said. 'I'm just trying to find out what talents I have. I want to grab every opportunity which comes my way, because I'm aware that the clock on this marriage is ticking away. And that when we part, I want to know who the real Rosa Corretti is and what she's capable of.' She stared at him in appeal, wanting him to understand. Praying that he would understand.

He picked up a file of papers. 'Then I must wish you well,' he said.

His words were dismissive and Rosa could feel her fingernails digging into the palms of her hands as he headed out of the room without even bothering to kiss her goodbye. Damn him and his prissy attitude, she raged silently as she heard the front door slam behind him.

Defiantly, she showered and dressed—and although she always felt at her thinnest in black, she remembered reading somewhere that you should never wear black in front of the camera. So she put on a green silk dress which brought out the emerald flecks in her eyes, and after a couple of cups of strong coffee she rang Arnaud Bertrand.

'Madame de la Désert,' he said slowly. 'This is a surprise.'

Rosa sucked in a deep breath, wondering if his offer had just been something meaningless which he'd tossed out during a lull in the dinner party conversation. 'Did you mean it when you suggested the screen test?'

There was a pause. 'But of course I meant it,' he said smoothly. 'I never say anything I don't mean. Can you come in for a test this afternoon?'

She thought afterwards that if he'd scheduled the test for the following week, then she might never have taken it. Maybe that was why he did it so quickly. All Rosa knew was that later that day she had the car drop her off at the TV studio, which was situated on the Avenue de la Grande Armée. The building overlooked the Arc de Triomphe and Arnaud told her that the iconic backdrop was often hired out to visiting foreign broadcasters.

'You don't seem too nervous,' he observed as he ran his eyes over her silky green dress.

Rosa gave an automatic smile. My husband doesn't want me to be here, she found herself wanting to say. I keep thinking about him, instead of the reason I'm here—and that's the reason why I'm not nervous. But she forced herself to push the memory of Kulal's face from her mind and to flash a bright smile at the TV executive instead. 'Surely nerves in front of the camera are a bad thing?'

'They certainly are.' Arnaud smiled back as he led her into the studio, where the lights were belting out a heat as fierce as a tropical sun. 'How good are you at ad-libbing?'

Rosa shrugged. 'I have no idea.'

They stood her in front of a giant green screen and explained that the weather report was one of the few things on television which didn't require an autocue. They told her that Paris was going to have sunny spells throughout the day, but that there would be scattered showers overnight. And then they asked her to talk about it on camera for thirty seconds, without a script.

She was a natural. Or at least, that's what they said afterwards, when she'd finished her slot. Just as the last few seconds were ticking away, she had turned to the camera and said, 'Sometimes I wish I was back in Sicily, where the sun always shines.' She'd heard shouts of laughter in her earpiece, and when Arnaud came to collect her from the studio floor, he'd been grinning—as if he'd just done something very clever.

He took her for coffee afterwards and told her that he'd been entirely correct and she did have that certain *je ne sais quoi* which made the camera love her. That it was a rare commodity but television gold. They couldn't offer her much at the moment, but they thought she'd be perfect for a daily 'novelty slot,' just after the lunchtime news.

She received the news with the enthusiasm she knew was expected of her, but when she left the café to slide into the back of the waiting limousine, all she could think of was how she was going to break it to Kulal. And wasn't that crazy? Because this was the chance of a lifetime—and wasn't this marriage supposed to be about freedom?

She had to start taking control. She was legally contracted to be Kulal's wife for another ten months and she certainly couldn't spend it moping around the place, wishing he felt stuff for her which he clearly didn't. If she didn't like something, then she needed to change it. And if she couldn't change him, then she needed to change herself. Couldn't she show her sheikh husband that it was possible to live in harmony, if they both made the effort? That they could compromise if they wanted to, just like any other modern couple.

She felt filled with a new sense of purpose as she took the elevator up to the apartment, and when Kulal arrived home she was waiting for him out on the terrace. She had mixed a drink of his favourite rosewater and pomegranate juice and his eyebrows rose speculatively as she held up the frosted pink jug. 'Drink?'

'A drink would be perfect,' he said, pulling off his jacket as he went out onto the terrace and joined her. He had thought that he would arrive home to an atmosphere, that she might be sulking in response to his obvious disapproval of her intention to ring Bertrand. But it seemed he had been wrong, for he'd never seen her looking quite so relaxed.

Sinking into one of the chairs, he watched as she bent to drop ice into the glass, his gaze resting on the curve of her bottom, and his heart began to accelerate as she handed him the drink. She was wearing her hair loose, just the way he liked it, and her flame-coloured dress accentuated her exotic colouring. Not only did she look good, but she was behaving in a way which pleased him since her attitude towards him was undeniably accommodating. Did this mean that she had reconsidered her rash statements of this morning? His gaze was approving as he took a sip of his drink and let out a rare sigh of contentment. 'I must applaud you, Rosa,' he said. 'For this is exactly how a man likes to be greeted after a hard day at the office.'

She waited until he'd put his drink down before she walked over and sat on his lap, looping her arms around his neck. 'And have you had a good day?'

'When you wriggle on my lap like that, it makes me forget—other than to say that it's getting better by the minute.'

She dipped her head forward and brushed her mouth over his. 'Is it?' she whispered.

He didn't answer, just put his hand up to anchor her head so that he could kiss her, and Rosa felt the shimmering of desire as if whispered over her skin. Her hands reached out to frame his face, her fingertips tracing the hard outline of his jaw and feeling the faint rasp of new growth there. Her fingers crept upwards, so that they could feel the hard slant of his cheekbones beneath the silken skin. And all during her tactile survey of his face, he continued to subject her to that sweetly drugging kiss so she was startled when, abruptly, he terminated it, pushing her away by a fraction so that he could look directly into her eyes.

'What's the matter?' she managed through dry lips. 'D-don't you want to make love?'

'You mean here?'

She wondered how best to respond. Up until now, Kulal had been the dominant one—not surprising given his vast experience and her complete lack of it. But she'd had a pretty intensive introduction to sex, hadn't she? Surely she'd had enough tuition for her to take the lead for once. Maybe that was what he wanted her to do.

'Of course here,' she whispered as she drifted her hand down to his groin, where he felt as hard as steel, and began to stroke him through the straining material of his trousers. 'I want you now. I can lift up my skirt and you can just slip inside me. No one need know a thing.'

The explicitness of her words excited yet shocked him and Kulal recognised a subtle shift in power between them as his body responded instantly to her touch. For a moment he allowed himself the fantasy of following through. Of allowing her floaty dress to conceal what was going on underneath. Of unzipping himself and pushing deep inside her honeyed heat. Gripping her wrist to arrest the movement of her captivating fingers, he put his face very close to hers. 'You don't think we can be seen?'

Rosa swallowed. 'This terrace is completely private.'

'Nowhere is completely private. There are long-range lenses and buildings all around which offer perfect vantage points.' His black eyes shot out black fire which blazed over her. 'Unless you are turned on by the thought that someone might be watching? Perhaps deep down you are longing for the kind of notoriety which would come from being the first woman to be photographed having sex with the sheikh?'

She stared at him, her heart beginning to pound painfully in her chest as she heard his unjust and harsh accusation. 'Is that what you think?' she whispered. 'Is that what you really think?'

'I don't know what to think. You are a constant series of surprises to me, Rosa—surprises which are becoming more apparent by the day. I had no idea, for example, that you were a frustrated television star.'

Shaking her head with indignation, she jumped off his lap and ran back inside the apartment but she quickly realised that he was following her. She could see his huge shadow dwarfing her and could hear him pressing a button so that the blinds floated silently down, leeching the room of all brightness and colour. She turned, seeing the look on his face.

'Don't,' she said, her heart quickening.

'Don't what?' he questioned. 'Don't continue what you started outside, only without the possibility of some paparazzi salivating over his camera? I thought that was what you were angling for, Rosa.'

The prospect of sex when he was looking as aroused as that made Rosa's body tremble for his touch, but pride made her shake her head with a sudden fury. 'Don't keep treating me like some mindless puppet who can't think for herself,' she said fiercely.

Her unexpected words made him halt in his tracks and he deliberately made his voice grow silky. 'But I'm just acting in your best interests. Surely you can see that it was unwise for us to be intimate outside, with the possibility that we could be seen by the paparazzi?'

'Yes, I can see that,' she said impatiently. 'But there are more diplomatic ways to tell me than by making me sound like some little tart who is seeking a crude kind of notoriety.'

There was a pause for a moment as he considered her words, his eyes travelling over her hurt and angry face before, slowly, he nodded. 'I'm sorry,' he said.

For a moment she thought she'd imagined it. She stared at him in disbelief. Had Kulal actually said *sorry*? 'You are?' she questioned cautiously.

'Of course I am.' He gave a heavy sigh. 'You've just given me what is probably the best homecoming I've ever had and all I've done is throw it back in your face.'

For a moment Rosa was too overcome to respond. Because Kulal had used an emotive word which could mean so much, especially to someone like him. Homecoming. Coming from a man whose own home life had been shattered by the death of his mother—wasn't that the greatest compliment he had ever paid her?

'It's okay,' she managed, but she was shaking with emotion all the same.

'I can be an ungrateful bastard at times,' he admitted as he stepped forward and took her in his arms. 'I guess part of me was still worried that you'd gone ahead and allowed yourself to take Bertrand's ridiculous suggestion seriously.'

Rosa stilled as the truth dawned on her. He thought she'd changed her mind. That she'd opted for the docile role of compliant wife—the role he obviously expected of her. That she was doing what he wanted her to do. She bit her lip. So what did she tell him? She could play safe by phoning Arnaud in the morning and telling him she'd changed her mind, thus guaranteeing harmony in her marriage. But at what cost? Was she going to have to subjugate everything about herself which didn't please this demanding sheikh? And for what? For him to turn around and leave her when the year was up, no matter what she did.

'You think it was a ridiculous suggestion?' she said carefully.

His lips gave the flicker of a smile. 'I'm afraid it was. I know what these people are like, Rosa. He wants to make sure that I give him permission to film in Zahrastan, which is why he chose to flatter you. People often try to target powerful men through their wives. Though if he was a little more discerning, he might have realised that his behaviour has angered me and that I dislike men fawning over you in such a way.'

For a moment Rosa was so outraged that she couldn't speak, even though his attitude was one she was used to. One she'd grown up with… He was making her sound like a racehorse, or a fancy car which another man was attempting to joyride. How dare he speak of her in such dismissive tones? She stared up at him, trying to stop her voice from trembling as she spoke. 'You think that's the only reason he showed interest in me—to get close to you?'

'Not the only reason, no. Any man with a pulse would want to get close to you in an altogether different way.'

Rosa nodded. 'So you wouldn't approve of me taking a screen test to appear on French TV?'

He gave a cynical smile. 'What do you think?'

'I think you'd better get your head around the fact that I've done exactly that.'

His eyes narrowed as she wrenched herself out of his arms. 'What are you talking about?'

'It's quite simple, Kulal. I went into the studios this afternoon and they gave me a try-out. They said I was very telegenic and so they've given me a slot.'

'They've given you a slot?' he repeated dangerously. 'On national television?'

'The very same. Only a tiny slot—it's true. But at least that means it won't be too disruptive to our lives.' She stared into the steely gleam of his black eyes. 'And next week I start presenting the weather report on the lunchtime news.'

CHAPTER ELEVEN

THE INTENSE LIGHT felt hot on her cheeks, but Rosa didn't mind. The brightness of the studio made some of the other presenters grow overheated, but not her. She was used to the glaring blaze of the Sicilian sun, so a few television lights weren't going to make her sweat! She flashed a wide smile as she finished her segment, reminding viewers to remember to pack an umbrella 'if you don't want your nice Parisian clothes to get wet!'

As always, her final comment made the crew smile, just as it would make the nation smile. In the instantly accessible world of television, Rosa had become a bit of a star, which was something she'd never envisaged.

Her rise to prominence in the national consciousness had all happened so quickly—and her popularity had been picked up by the press, during a quiet summer when there wasn't very much news. Newspaper analysts had been quick to question 'Why Rosa?' because she wasn't an obvious choice to be a pin-up. France had a recognised template for beauty, and Rosa didn't fit it. She was curvy and she didn't wear black. Her clothes were the colours of an exotic bird's plumage and she wore flowers in her hair. She should have been invisible in a place where thinness reigned supreme and women worshiped at the altar of high fashion. But people liked her. Men liked her because she was the stuff of forbidden fantasy, and their wives liked her because they didn't perceive her as a threat. French department stores had reported an increased demand for colour-blocked clothes. A glossy magazine had even urged its readers to throw away their diet books and 'channel your inner Rosa.'

Then had come the discovery that before her marriage to one of the world's most powerful men, Rosa had been a Corretti—and all hell had broken loose. Suddenly, she had become even more sought-after. The studio bosses asked her to do an extra weather slot on the highly prestigious breakfast show, but she'd said no, because who in their right mind would want to get up at three in the morning? Even farmers slept for longer than that! Requests for interviews began to pour in but she told Arnaud to refuse them all. She knew her family would go ballistic if journalists started to pry into its chequered history. And she knew that any more exposure would make Kulal even angrier than he already was....

'Just why are you doing this, Rosa?' he had demanded one morning, just before he'd stormed off to his office. 'Pursuing a useless career as a weather announcer? Telling people what they can already read on their cellphones!'

Those had been his actual words—words which had been intended to wound and which had hit their target full-on. Rosa had swallowed down the hurt she'd felt.

If only he had given her a few crumbs of praise, then she might have refused the offer of the Friday teatime slot in addition to her regular lunchtime one. If he'd told her that her French accent was flawless—which was what everyone else said—or that she'd managed to make women who felt bad about their bodies feel better about themselves, then she might have cut back or even deferred her fledgling career until after the marriage had ended.

But Kulal wasn't in the business of praising. He was in the business of making her feel like she had overstepped the mark. As if she had no right to do anything with her life if it dared to interfere with his.

She arrived home late one Friday after a meeting with Arnaud, and when she rushed into the apartment Kulal was standing waiting for her. His gaze ran over her, his black eyes lingering on the rose in her hair, and she saw the almost imperceptible twist of his lips. The fresh flower had become her 'trademark' and was provided by the studio before every show, but she'd forgotten she was wearing it and it was now probably wilting.

'You're late,' he observed caustically. 'And your face is covered in make-up.'

She touched her fingertips to her cheek and they came away the deep bronze colour of the heavy studio foundation. 'I wanted to get away as quickly as possible.' She drew in a deep breath and smiled. 'To get home to you.'

'That's very considerate of you, but have you forgotten that we were supposed to have been going out tonight?'

'Out?' She looked at him blankly, and then clapped her hand over her mouth in horror. 'Cocktails at the French Embassy!' she breathed. 'Oh, Kulal—it slipped my mind completely. But it's not too late, is it? We can still go.'

'It is too late, and the sheikh is never late,' he snapped. 'It would be an unspeakable diplomatic breach!'

'I'm sorry.'

With a growing feeling of frustration, Kulal stared at her, wanting to kiss her and yet wanting to rail against her all at the same time. Did she think that this situation she had manufactured was in any way acceptable to him? That he would ever tolerate being consigned to second place in her life? 'Obviously you're having difficulty fitting me into your busy schedule, Rosa.'

'That's not fair. My work hardly impacts on your life at all. Why didn't you remind me this morning?'

'Because it is not my place to remind you!' he bit out as he found himself longing for the days when she'd always been there, waiting. When he'd needed to do nothing but open the front door before she would be nestling in his arms—a package of curvaceous warmth and eager kisses. He remembered the way they used to sit on the terrace and watch the sun going down, before the lights of the city brought it to vivid life once more. 'You think I have nothing better to do than to act as your social secretary?'

'No, Kulal,' she said tiredly. 'I don't think that.'

She went into the bathroom to shower away the heavy make-up, and when she returned she thought that his mood was better. But maybe that was because she was

wearing a light summer dress which came to just above
the knee. She could see the instinctive gleam of his
black eyes as he pulled her into his arms and kissed her.
One kiss led to another, and then another—and sex always made Kulal feel better. Actually, it usually did the
same for her, but today she was left feeling strangely
empty as she lay in his arms afterwards.

The weather that weekend was amazing—the sky
a clear and vaulted blue and the sunshine bright and
golden as it shone down on one of the world's most
beautiful cities. They spent Saturday morning in one
of the flea markets, followed by a stroll around the
Tuileries after lunch. Most of Sunday took place in bed.

'Doesn't this feel fantastic?' murmured Kulal as he
traced lazy circles all over her stomach. 'And don't you
feel fantastic—all soft and sensual?'

Sensation shivered over her. Yes, it felt fantastic. It
always did. Rosa felt her heart clench, knowing that she
was going to miss this when the year was up. Could she
ever imagine being physically intimate with another
man like this? She shuddered. Never in a million years!
Could she imagine a life without Kulal full stop? A sudden darkness crept into her heart as she nestled closer
to his naked body. 'Do you ever think about what's
going to happen when we dissolve the marriage?' she
questioned.

'There's no point,' Kulal said, but her question had
destroyed the mood and he rolled away from her. He had
learnt never to project—even though sometimes he saw
the dark wings of the future flapping ominously on the

periphery of his vision. 'We made a decision and we're sticking to it. What's to think about?'

Rosa watched as he got out of bed and headed for the door, returning a few minutes later with two glasses of white wine. She took hers and began to sip at it, but her thoughts were troubled and she couldn't seem to shake them off. She'd told herself right from the beginning that she didn't believe in love. That she wasn't looking for love—but wasn't it peculiar how sometimes love seemed to come looking for you? How it could creep up on you and wrap its velvet fingers around your heart without you realising—even when the man in question could be stubborn, demanding and autocratic? Reason seemed to have no effect on her volatile emotions and she knew why.

She had fallen in love with her sheikh husband even though that was the last thing which either of them wanted.

No further mention was made of the future which meant that by Monday morning the atmosphere between them was serene. The missed party at the embassy was long forgotten and the goodbye kiss they shared as Kulal left for the office was lingering.

'I wish you didn't have to go,' she said.

'I wish that too.'

She wriggled her body against him. 'And I promise I won't ever be late again.'

Kulal gave an odd kind of smile before brushing his lips over hers one final time. 'Let's hope not.'

Rosa went to the studios, but as the crew began to mike her up for her segment, she thought that they didn't seem as chatty as usual. And afterwards, when she went to the dressing room to wipe off her make-up, there was a knock at the door.

It was Arnaud Bertrand and she raised her eyebrows in surprise, because he didn't usually come to her dressing room.

'Have you got a minute?' he said awkwardly. 'I need to talk to you.'

'Talk away.' She smiled at him in the mirror. 'Do you mean here, or would you rather go next door and we can get some coffee?'

'No, here is fine.' He looked slightly uncomfortable, his hands digging deep into the pockets of his trousers. 'Rosa, there's no easy way to say this, but I'm afraid we're pulling your slot.'

She turned round. 'What do you mean?'

'The bosses have decided that it's no longer working.'

She gazed at him blankly. 'But…I don't understand. You told me that everyone loved the feature. You said that you hadn't had so much fan mail since Johnny Depp gave that interview.'

He didn't quite meet her eyes. 'I'm afraid it's out of my hands.'

Rosa frowned as her heart began to pound loudly in her chest. 'Something's happened, hasn't it?'

Arnaud looked even more uncomfortable. 'Nothing has happened.'

'You're not a very good liar, Arnaud.' Her eyes narrowed. 'Has this got something to do with my husband?'

'I can't—'

'Oh, I think you can. Tell me!' she said, and then softened her voice. 'Please.'

There was a moment of silence before he gave a sigh of resignation. 'Okay, I'll tell you—but you didn't hear it from me. It does have something to do with your husband. In fact, it has everything to do with him. He's threatened to pull out of the documentary if we don't stop...' He shrugged his shoulders. '"Monopolising my wife" was how I think he phrased it.'

Rosa flinched to think that any man could be old-fashioned and chauvinistic enough to march up to a bunch of TV executives and tell them something like that. 'And you're willing to just cave in?' she questioned heatedly. 'To let this go just because you want to make some damned documentary about his country?'

Arnaud shook his head. 'It's not just the documentary!' he said. 'It's everything else. Your husband is a powerful man, Rosa—not just in Paris, but pretty much everywhere else. And you don't make enemies of men like that.'

The realisation of what Kulal had done suddenly hit her and Rosa felt sick. Her heart was pounding and her chest felt so tight that Arnaud reached out towards her in alarm.

'Mon dieu!' he exclaimed. 'But your face is like chalk! Sit down, and I will fetch you some water.'

But she shook her head. 'I don't want anything,' she said fiercely. But that wasn't quite true, was it? She wanted to regain her honour and her pride and there was only one way she was going to do that.

She flipped through her address book before going

outside, ignoring Kulal's official limousine which was waiting for her just as it always was. Quickly, she darted down one of the side streets and felt a flash of triumph as she gave her bodyguard the slip, before clicking onto the map section of her phone. Her footsteps were rapid as she walked to the sixteenth *arrondissement* until she had reached the ornate nineteenth-century building which housed Kulal's foundation.

She realised that it was the first time she'd ever been inside the building and she saw the receptionist's look of shock as she walked in.

'I'm Rosa,' she said automatically, knowing how hot and dishevelled she must look after her dash across the city.

'You are the sheikh's wife,' breathed the receptionist, her look of shock deepening. 'And I have seen you on the television.'

'Where is he?' Rosa asked quietly. 'Where is the sheikh?'

'I'm afraid he is in a meeting, and I'll have to—'

'Where is he?' Rosa repeated, and then spotted the staircase on the opposite side of the lobby. He would be at the top of the building—of course he would—because powerful people always chose their vantage points up high, so that they could look down on the rest of the world. She ran up the stairs, two at a time, until there was nowhere left to go and she passed another receptionist who had clearly been warned that trouble was on the way. The woman shot a horrified glance in the direction of a set of double doors and that look told Rosa everything she needed to know.

She burst in through the doors to see a huge table with lots of men in suits sitting around it and they all looked up as she appeared. But only one man dominated the room with his powerful presence. A man with black eyes and dark skin and the demeanour of a desert warrior, despite the sleek outlines of his Italian suit. He was getting to his feet and all the men were looking up at him in alarm, before staring at her again.

'Rosa,' he said in a voice she'd never heard him use before. 'What an unexpected pleasure.'

'I want to talk to you.'

'Can't this wait until later?' he questioned. 'Because as you can see, I'm in the middle of a meeting which has taken some time and trouble to organise.'

'No, it can't wait!' she flared, hearing the onlookers draw in a collective shocked breath and she recognised then that people spent their lives appeasing Kulal and giving him exactly what he wanted. And how could that be good for him? 'So either you get rid of them now, or we're going to have an audience while I put to you a few very pertinent questions!'

'Gentlemen, looks like we're done here,' said Kulal, but Rosa couldn't miss the unmistakable glint of anger in his eyes.

They stood in silence while all the men filed out, and when the door had been closed, Kulal looked at her and she saw that the glint had become a quietly smouldering blaze.

'So, are you going to give me some sort of explanation for this unwarranted intrusion?'

'Are you?' she retorted.

'I'm not in the mood for riddles, Rosa!'

'Aren't you? Well then, let me spell this one out for you! Did you…' She gripped on to the back of a chair to steady herself, aware that her voice sounded all croaky. Kulal gestured towards the water jug on the table but she shook her head furiously, as if he was offering her a beaker of poison. 'Did you put a stop to my weather slot?'

There was a moment of silence.

'I want the truth, Kulal! Did you?'

He shrugged. 'I'm no television executive,' he said. 'It's not within my power to do something like that.'

'But it's certainly within your power to threaten to withdraw permission for filming to begin in Zahrastan, isn't it? And it's certainly within your power to lean heavily on investors, if that's what it takes. Is that what you did, Kulal?'

He looked at her for a long moment and then he gave a curt nod, as if he had just come to a decision. 'Yes, I did it—and you want to know why? Because I don't think it's such a heinous crime for a husband to want to see more of his wife. A wife who is only mine for a year! Why should I wish to share her with millions of viewers and the people who read those dreadful magazines?'

Rosa's throat was so tight that it felt as if it had an invisible cord clenched around it and it took a moment or two before she could respond with any degree of clarity. 'So you just stormed in and took control? You decided that because you didn't like it, that you would change it. Because even if it is only for a year, you don't really want a wife, do you, Kulal? What you want is a doll— a doll you can play with whenever you want. Someone that you can dress and undress and put to bed. Something you can walk away from in the morning, knowing exactly where your little doll has been all day, because one of your damned bodyguards has been tracking her.'

At this moment, an urgent-sounding buzzer on his desk began to go off and Kulal leaned over to press his finger on it. 'Yes...?'

Rosa recognised the frantic tones of the bodyguard who had been assigned to her that day. 'Boss, I've lost the princess.'

'Don't worry, I've found her.'

'You see!' She glared at him as he clicked off the connection. 'You even make me sound like a doll—or a package which has inadvertently gone missing.'

'As my wife you require a security issue!' he flared. 'You cannot deny that, Rosa!'

'I'm not here to talk about my security!' she flared back. 'I'm here to talk about the fact that you heavy-handedly put an end to my burgeoning TV career and you didn't even have the courtesy to tell me!'

His mouth tightened. 'And is this television slot really so important to you?'

She shook her head as hot, infuriating tears began to spring to her eyes. 'You're missing the point,' she said. 'I left one life because people expected me to behave a certain way. I was trapped and controlled and told what to do every minute of the day. And you're doing exactly the same thing! You promised me freedom and independence and you've given me the opposite.'

'You'll get your freedom and independence when

the marriage is over,' he said, his hands clenching into tight fists.

'And it'll be too late by then,' she said, and now her voice was trembling. 'Kulal, you're making this very difficult for me. You don't want a wife with a career, but neither do you want a wife who you'll let close enough to love you. Can't you see that I'm between a rock and a hard place here?'

His eyes flicked over her and he steeled himself against the tears which were sparking so brightly in her eyes. He remembered the night of their honeymoon when she'd sobbed against his bare chest as she'd told him about her mother's betrayal and a shiver of something dark and empathetic had whispered over his skin. But the intensity of those feelings had made him feel raw and vulnerable—and hadn't he vowed that he would never allow himself to feel that way again? He drew a deep breath as he stared at the flyaway mess of her dark hair and the flushed sheen of her face. 'Can we discuss this later?' he said. 'When you've calmed down a little, and maybe had a chance to brush your hair?'

Rosa almost choked with frustration, until she realised that maybe this was exactly what she needed—to hear him utter the truth in all its stark brutality. Get out of his life, she told herself. Get out now while you still can—before he sees just how much he has hurt you. She sucked in a deep breath. 'I'd like that drink now, if you don't mind.'

He poured her a glass of water. 'I can ring for some ice, if you like.'

'No, thanks.' Her smile was wan as she gulped down

the tepid liquid. 'Tell me, Kulal, do you always get exactly what it is you want?'

Her words took him back. He thought about what they used to say about him in Zahrastan. *What Kulal wants, Kulal gets.* But not always. Not the one time when it really mattered, when his heart had been shattered into a thousand little pieces—and he was damned if he was going to risk that happening again. 'You're talking in riddles again,' he said.

'Am I? Yet you're a highly intelligent man. I'm sure you can understand exactly what I'm talking about, if only you'd let yourself. But there's no need to look so worried. The discussion's over and I'm going now.'

'And we'll talk about it some more tonight.'

'Of course we will.' The lie came easily to her lips, just as it had come to his. Because Kulal had no intention of talking about this any more. She knew that. The decision had been made—his decision—and he would just expect her to get used to it. To go along with it, like a good little girl. She could imagine the scene which would enfold tonight. The hungry kiss, heightened by all the tension, and then a session of lovemaking powerful enough to push any nagging doubts from her mind. Well, not any more. Because Rosa Corretti was through with being manipulated. She was going to start taking control of her life, as of now.

She looked up at him, but it felt as if her face might split in two with the effort it took to smile. 'I'll see you later.'

CHAPTER TWELVE

KULAL SHOULD HAVE felt better after Rosa had gone, leaving him alone in his vast office. He told himself that she needed to understand that they'd made a deal and that he wasn't prepared for her to start reneging on it. He hadn't signed up for someone who wouldn't be there when he needed her. Until he reminded himself fiercely that he didn't actually need anybody—because need was dangerous. It made you dependent and it made you weak.

He pulled a pile of papers towards him and started to read them, but the afternoon passed by much too slowly. He knew that he could have left the office any time he pleased, since he didn't have any more meetings planned, and even if he did, he could always cancel them. But he didn't go home. Why should he go home early to a woman who didn't appreciate him?

What Kulal wanted, Kulal got.

The words stayed irritatingly in his head, like an advertising jingle which wouldn't go away, and his temple was throbbing by the time he took the elevator up to the apartment. As the doors slid open he wondered what was the best way to handle what had happened earlier. He could quietly take Rosa aside and tell her that he wouldn't tolerate a repeat of such a hysterical scene but mightn't that make her stubborn? Mightn't the argument then continue into the evening, when he had plenty of other things he'd rather be doing with her than arguing?

And he had made his point, hadn't he? He had won. There would be no more missed cocktail parties, nor would they be disturbed by any phone calls from the infernal Bertrand. There would be no more business colleagues telling him that their wives had seen a picture of his wife in a magazine.

The apartment was strangely silent—there wasn't even any music playing—and Kulal walked through to the drawing room to see if Rosa was out on the terrace. But the French windows were closed and there was no sign of her with a forgiving smile on her beautiful lips as she sashayed towards him in one of her vibrant dresses.

'Rosa?' The word echoed around the vast rooms like something shouted into a tunnel. 'Rosa!' he called once more, but there was no reply.

He told himself that she must have just gone out for a while. But she didn't do that, did she—because where would she go? The galleries were shut for the day and there was no need for her to perform the multiple tasks which fell to other, less exalted women. She didn't need to shop or to cook or to clean. She was a princess and that was why she needed to behave like a princess!

A faint frown creased his brow as he remembered the frustration on her face when she'd confronted him today. The anger spitting green and golden sparks from her dark eyes. He remembered the messy spill of her hair and her shiny face—a look which was worlds apart from the usual sleek grooming of his former lovers. He thought about the wilted rose tucked behind her ear, and a wave of lust so strong washed over him that for a moment he just stood very still and closed his eyes.

He was just about to phone her, when he walked past the dining room and saw the cream-coloured envelope which was lying on the oak table and his heart missed a beat. He stared at it for a moment, and when he walked over and picked it up, he noticed almost impartially that his fingers weren't quite steady.

It was the first thing she'd ever written to him and, judging by the tone, she intended it to be her last.

'Kulal,' it read. Not 'dear' Kulal or 'darling' Kulal— or any of the other sweet things she had sometimes whispered to him when he was deep inside her body— but just his name, stark and emotionless, just like the words which followed.

I imagine you'll be pleased to discover that I've gone, especially after that rather unfortunate scene at your office today. I'm sorry if I embarrassed you in front of your colleagues, but please be assured that it won't ever happen again, because I'm leaving and I think you'll agree that's best.

Since I won't be honouring our marriage contract, you can tear up the pre-nup. All I'm taking are my wedding and engagement rings, which you told me were mine to keep. I'll probably sell them and set myself up with somewhere to rent, before I look for a job. And one day—who knows?—I may be able to pay you back for them, in full.

Thank you for all that you have taught me, which turns out to have been a lot more than just about sex.

I hope you can find it in yourself to be happy and I wish you nothing but good things.
Yours ever,
Rosa.

'No!' He felt a dry and tearing pain as he crumpled the piece of paper tightly in his hand and it fell in a ball and bounced soundlessly on the table while Kulal dug his phone from his pocket.

He punched out her number, unsurprised when it went straight to voicemail and a curiously flat-sounding Rosa said that she would return the call as quickly as possible. Which was clearly not going to happen. He left two messages before letting out another howl of rage, tempted to hurl the damned phone against the wall. And he remembered Rosa telling him she'd done just that when she'd run from Sicily, when she'd wanted to cut off all communication with her family. And now she was running from him. He had gone from his privileged position as her husband and her lover to being cast out in the cold. And he had no one to blame but himself. He had convinced himself that he was fearless and strong and yet he had been so scared of dealing with his emotions that he had built a wall around them. He had allowed a tragedy in his past to blight any possibility of a future and he had pushed away the woman he loved.

A wave of pain hit him. A pain so intense that it felt

like an iron fist clenching its way around his heart. Where was she?

He dialled his chief bodyguard. 'I want you to find someone for me,' he clipped out.

'Anyone you like, boss. Who is it?'

There was a pause as, for one brief moment, Kulal confronted his own fierce pride and knew that he was going to have to let it go. Who cared if his bodyguards discovered that his wife had left him? Who cared about anything other than getting Rosa back again?

'My wife.'

'The princess has gone?' questioned the bodyguard in surprise.

'Yes, the princess has gone!' snapped Kulal. 'Because your people weren't doing their job properly. They let her leave the studios unguarded and now she's managed to give everyone the slip. And if you value your future you'll find out where she is by sunset tomorrow.'

They did better than that—they had located Rosa by the following afternoon and Kulal was astonished to discover that she'd flown back to Sicily.

Sicily?

She'd told him she'd never go back there! She'd told him that no way was she going to get involved with her dysfunctional family ever again.

'Is she staying with her family?'

'No, boss. She's all alone in a beach house on the eastern side of the island.'

Kulal nodded. 'Prepare the plane,' he said grimly.

It occurred to him when his jet touched down several hours later that her powerful family might have attempted to try to stop him from entering the country, but he was wrong. It also occurred to him that maybe he should have waited until the next morning to see her, for the sun was already beginning to sink in the sky as his waiting car drove away from the airfield. But for the first time in his life he couldn't bear the thought of waiting—no matter how much bigger a psychological advantage that would be.

Eventually, the car bumped to a halt and the driver pointed to a solitary beach house in the distance, barely visible through all the trees and shrubbery. It was in part of a nature reserve and the area was impassable to all cars. Kulal found himself thinking that the gleaming limousine wouldn't have stood a chance of negotiating that narrow path. He told his driver to go and he told the car containing the accompanying bodyguards to follow, waving aside their protests with a flat and implacable movement of his hand.

'I don't want anyone else here,' he said fiercely. 'Now go.'

'But, boss—'

'Go!'

He stood and watched the powerful vehicles roar away to make sure they obeyed him. Large clouds of dust puffed around their gleaming paintwork as the two cars became little black dots in the distance. And suddenly, he felt an unexpected wave of liberation. It was, he realised, a long time since he'd gone anywhere without being shadowed by one of the guards who had been part of his life for as long as he could remember.

For the first time, he allowed himself to look properly at his surroundings, taking in a deep breath of the scented air. It smelt of lemon and pine and he could hear the massed choir of the cicadas echoing over the hills. The baked vegetation was surprisingly green—with flowers dotted here and there—and in the distance he could see the deep cobalt of the sea. He stared down at his feet and some instinct made him slip off his loafers and carry them.

The warm sand was gritty between his toes and as he walked along the narrow path he felt that sense of freedom again. Was that because for the first time in his life he was following his heart? Because in this moment he was no longer a royal prince and sheikh, but simply a man who had come to make amends with his woman.

The beach house which lay ahead of him was modest, just a one-storey building with a wide, wooden veranda looking out to sea. The beauty lay in its position—the matchless view and the solitude—and suddenly Kulal wondered what he was going to do if Rosa wasn't there. How would she react if she came back later to find him waiting for her? Would she turn the might of the Corretti family against an estranged husband she could rightly accuse of stalking her?

He didn't care. Let the Correttis come. Let them all come. He wasn't going anywhere until he'd looked into Rosa's eyes and told her what she needed to hear.

He moved silently, for at heart he was a child of the desert, taught how to blend into whichever landscape he inhabited. He thought fleetingly that Sicily was as beautiful as everything he'd ever heard about it, and that he'd like the chance to explore it further. And then he saw her and his footsteps halted, so that he stood perfectly still.

Sitting at the far end of the veranda, her legs dangling over the side, she was shaded by an umbrella pine tree but was wearing a sun hat as an extra precaution. The hat looked new and was made of straw—its crown festooned with a bright mass of orange and pink silk flowers, which matched her sundress. He could feel a lump forming in his throat as he watched her staring intently out at the sea. He wanted to stand there all day watching her but he thought that she might turn around and be startled. More than startled.

'Rosa,' he said softly.

For a moment Rosa didn't move, telling herself it was like one of those fantasies which schoolgirls sometimes concocted. The ones where the object of their affections would suddenly be spirited in front of them, no matter how unlikely that scenario would be.

'Rosa,' said the voice again.

Her fingernails dug into her thighs. Bad enough that she should be without him—but did she also have to suffer auditory hallucinations which were designed to torment her?

Slowly, she turned her head and her breath froze in her throat. She could hear the loud thunder of her heart as he held up the palms of his hands, like someone in an old cowboy film, admitting surrender.

'I didn't mean to startle you,' he said.

'Well, you did.' She tried not to feast her eyes on him, but it was impossible. How could you not look at him and keep on looking, when he seemed like a dark and sculpted god who had just been planted in the Sicilian landscape? He was wearing pale linen trousers and a pale silk shirt—the sleeves rolled up to reveal his dark, hair-roughened arms. From this distance she couldn't really see his expression, but as he grew nearer she noticed that his feet were bare. Kulal walking in public in bare feet? She looked over his shoulder to the landscape behind. And where were his bodyguards?

It didn't matter. None of those questions were relevant because he was no longer part of her life. She'd escaped from him and his controlling ways. Nothing had changed. Only the externals. She had left him and his home in Paris and she was starting a new life for herself. It wasn't going to be easy because she still wanted him, but she was going to do it. She needed to do it.

He was closer now. He was stepping down onto the veranda so that she could see the dark gleam of his eyes and she knew she ought to tell him to just go away and leave her alone, but in that moment she discovered that her sense of curiosity was stronger than her sense of self-preservation.

'What are you doing here?' she questioned, trying to inject just the right note of careless sarcasm into her voice. 'No, don't tell me—you've come to try to bring your little doll back to Paris. Is it time to brush her hair and put her back into her shiny box?'

Kulal stood looking down at her, reading the hurt and anger on her upturned face as he thought of all the inducements he could use to get her to return to Paris with him. He thought of all the things he could say to try to persuade her. Things she probably wouldn't believe—

and who could blame her? And he didn't know where
to begin, because this was all new to him. He clenched
his fists as all his buttoned-up feelings demanded to
be set free, but habit made him want to resist. Damn
it, why shouldn't he resist? There was a reason why he
had put all his emotions into cold storage and it was a
good reason. If you didn't allow yourself to feel things,
then you couldn't get hurt.

But suddenly, it was no longer working. Whatever
had protected him in the past was failing to protect
him now for the pain in his heart was very real and
very raw. He moved across the terrace and sat down
beside her and he saw her body tense. For a moment
there was silence.

'I miss you,' he said.

She shook her head. 'No, you don't. You just think
you do. It's because I was the one who walked away and
your pride is hurt. You'll get over it.'

'No, I won't get over it,' he said. 'I don't think I could,
even if I wanted to. And I don't. I just want you back
in my life because I love you, Rosa.' The words left his
mouth in a breathless rush, but his voice was shaking
with emotion as he finished his quiet declaration. 'I
love you in a way I never thought I could love anyone,
and that's the truth.'

Rosa could feel a horrible lump forming in her throat
and the betraying flavour of salt in her mouth but she
wasn't going to cry. Damn him—she wasn't going to
cry. And she wasn't going to listen to his empty words
either. He might have all the real power—the social and
the economic power which came with his royal title—

but she had power too. She had the power to live her life as she wanted to. Without pain and without heartbreak. She shook her head. 'It's too late, Kulal.'

'No!' In the growing darkness his word was fervent as it rang out on the still, Sicilian air. 'Don't tell me that we don't all deserve a second chance when we screw up so spectacularly. And I recognise that I've behaved like a fool. You said in my office that you wanted to love me but that I wouldn't let you close enough. But I'm letting you close now. Are you telling me that your feelings for me have changed, Rosa? That twenty-four hours have altered the situation so radically?'

She tried not to be affected by the look of raw pain on his face as he spoke, but it was the hardest thing she'd ever had to do. Because of course she hadn't stopped loving him. Love wasn't something you could just turn on and off, like a tap. She wanted to take him into her arms and cradle him. She wanted to lose her heartache in the sweetness of his kiss—but what good would that do? This is short-term pain for long-term gain, she told herself fiercely. He just needs to win at everything and that's why he wants you back.

'I'm not the kind of woman you need, Kulal,' she said quietly. 'You need someone you can dominate. Someone who will do exactly what you want her to do. Some women might call that being masterful but I call it being a control freak and I'm afraid that I can't live like that. Not any more.'

His body tensed. 'You can have your TV slot back!'

'No!' Frustratedly, she shook her hands in the air.

'You don't understand! This is nothing to do with my TV slot.'

'But isn't that what drove you away?'

She stared at him. 'That was the final straw, yes. But what really drove me away was the fundamental inequality of our relationship. I don't want to live with someone who won't let me do something—so that only when I push and push will he change his mind and give me his permission. I'm a grown-up, Kulal. I don't need anyone's permission to live my life. Not yours, nor my family's. I've had that for too many years and I don't want it any more.'

He saw the sudden fierceness on her face. 'Why did you come back to Sicily?' he questioned suddenly. 'When you told me you would never return.'

There was silence for a moment as Rosa mulled over his question. 'Because I thought about something you said and realised that you were right. That I had no right to try to fix you, when my own life was so unresolved,' she said. 'I knew I needed to speak to my brothers and to my mother. Especially my mother. I needed to hear her side of the story. I needed to hear what made her betray my dad with his own brother, but then I had to let it go. Because it's her life, not mine.'

'And what did she say?'

'I'm meeting her for coffee tomorrow morning.' She nearly said, 'I'll let you know,' until she realised that she wouldn't, because tomorrow he would be gone from here. She wanted him gone from here. She needed him gone from here.

He saw the new strain on her face and his heart

twisted. 'I'm sorry for what you've been through with your family, Rosa—'

'Yes, I know that,' she put in, hating the betraying little crack which seemed to have crept into her voice. 'And that was one of the things I first loved about you— that you defied all my expectations. That once you'd got over the shock of my parentage, you supported me. And I was so grateful to you for that, Kulal. I thought you would judge me negatively, but you didn't. And then, when you opened up to me on the night of our wedding, I felt something like hope about the future. It felt as if two people who had been damaged could find comfort and solace in each other. But then you clammed up— and even though there were moments when I felt as if a real passion and friendship was there, it was as if you wanted to keep it locked away from me.'

'And I did,' he said slowly, her words unlocking a conundrum he'd never really understood until now. He stared at her. 'I guess I was terrified of getting too close to anyone. It felt like too much of a risk. Can you understand that, Rosa?'

She nodded as she heard the flicker of uncertainty in his voice and suddenly her man of steel seemed soft and vulnerable and she couldn't seem to stop her heart from reaching out to him. 'Of course I can understand,' she said. 'Your mother was torn away from you in a way which left you heartbroken. Worse still was that you blamed yourself. You still do.'

'You know why I blame myself,' he said quietly. 'You know what happened that day.'

'But you're not even sure about the facts, are you?'

she whispered. 'You've refused to look at the post-mortem report or speak to the doctors.' She saw him flinch but she knew she had to carry on. Because even though Kulal was no longer a small boy locked in a nightmare of guilt and loss, he was a man still suffering as a consequence of that day, and he would continue to suffer unless he confronted it. 'I think you should go back to Zahrastan and find out the truth. You told me that your mother was suffering from headaches prior to the picnic. Well, maybe the fall was a result of that. Maybe she would have died anyway—or maybe she wouldn't. You have to know, Kulal. You can't keep living your life burdened by guilt and neither can you keep avoiding risk, just because it's safer that way. You have to learn to take a chance—on me, yes, but more importantly, on yourself.'

He swallowed, struggling to cope with the new and very powerful feelings which were beginning to emerge. And he wondered if it really was too late. 'I'll go,' he said. 'And I'll face whatever truth awaits me there—but before I do, there's something you need to know. Something I never told you before, but which I should have done.' There was a pause as he looked down at the soft parting of her lips. 'That the first time I saw you, you spoke to something in my heart. I looked across that crowded nightclub, little realising that I was about to meet a woman who would change just about everything.'

'Kulal—'

'And that is why I am asking you—with all the earnestness at my command—can we please try again?

Because I love you, Rosa, and I want to be a real husband to you—in every sense of the word.'

She was swallowing frantically but it was no good, because the tears which had begun welling up in her eyes had begun to trickle down her cheeks. And she saw from the sudden darkening of his features that he was in danger of misinterpreting those tears and that's when she stopped fighting her own feelings. She gave in to what she'd been wanting to do all along and flung her arms around his neck, her face wet as she pressed her lips to his.

'Yes,' she said, whispering the words directly into his mouth. 'Yes in every language that I speak—and in yours too, which I have yet to learn. Yes, because I love you too—even though I tried to tell myself that I was crazy to love you. But I couldn't stop myself, no matter how hard I tried. And I want to spend the rest of my life loving you back, but only if you promise never to lock me out of your heart again.'

'I promise,' he said fiercely. 'Now will you please just kiss me properly before I go out of my mind?'

Her lips were pressing hard against his almost before he'd finished the sentence but the kiss felt different. It felt like a statement—and a seal. It felt almost life-changing. And maybe it was. She smiled as if she'd suddenly understood the world's best-kept secret as Kulal stood up and lifted her into his arms, before carrying her into the small, wooden house.

Because didn't everyone always say that true love had the power to transform?

EPILOGUE

THE AL-DIMASHQI PALACE shone in the late-afternoon light, rising up from the stark landscape like a beautiful fairy-tale castle in the distance and Rosa peered out of the car window with a fast-growing feeling of excitement. She had been longing to visit the desert kingdom of Zahrastan and now the moment was here at last. She could see turrets and domes and the tantalising glimmer of water in among the rose gardens and she gave a little sigh of anticipation.

Kulal squeezed her hand. 'Nervous?' he questioned.

'A bit.' She turned to look at him. 'I'm terrified your brother won't like me.'

'What's not to like?' His eyes were soft as he studied her. 'You are the woman who has tamed the tearaway sheikh. The proud Sicilian beauty my people are longing to meet.' He lifted her hand to his lips and kissed it. 'And the woman who has captured my heart so completely.'

'Well, when you put it like that.' She brushed her fingertips over his mouth, but her next words were hesitant. 'And how do you feel about coming back, Kulal? I mean, really.'

Kulal was quiet for a moment while he considered

her question. This was his second trip to Zahrastan in
as many months. The first time he had come alone and
it had been a trip of necessity, not of pleasure. He had
gone to the hospital in the capital, where his mother
had been taken following her fall. Assiduously, he had
forced himself to read through all the records and then
had spoken to the medical director, who'd been a very
junior doctor at the time.

Vividly, Kulal remembered flying back to Paris.
He remembered the hopeful expression on Rosa's face
and the way it had become wary when he told her that
the tests had proved inconclusive. That he still didn't
know whether his mother's death had been caused by
the fall or by some pre-existing condition. But that it
was okay. He'd told her that too. It was all okay. The
past had happened and there was nothing he could do
to change it. All he had was the present—the glorious
present, with his loving wife, who had taught him so
much, by his side.

'I feel joy,' he said simply. 'And gratitude. That in
finding you, I could find myself and learn to live in a
way I never thought possible. And I'm looking forward
to the celebrations.'

'Me too,' she said. 'Though I've had my reservations
about the guest list.'

'Well, don't. I utterly forbid it. And I don't know why
you're giggling like that, Rosa—because I do!'

He tightened his hand around hers. They were here
in Zahrastan because the king wanted to throw a big
party for his brother and his Sicilian bride. Kulal's former fiancée, Ayesha, would be there, with the Tuscan

nobleman she had surprised everyone by marrying after Kulal had 'freed' her from their engagement. His lips curved. How life could constantly surprise! Rosa's family had also been invited and most of them were coming. There would doubtless be friction, though hopefully the august surroundings of the Al-Dimashqi palace might inject a little calm into the sometimes overexuberant nature of the Corretti clan.

And if it didn't? If there were noisy scenes and tears, and make-ups and break-ups? So what. What would be, would be. Kulal had learnt that there was much in life he couldn't control. He'd learnt that taking a risk was sometimes as necessary to life as breathing itself. He touched his hand to the gleaming crown of his wife's dark hair and smiled as he bent to kiss her.

And he'd learnt that love was the most necessary thing of all.

* * * * *

*Read on for an exclusive interview
with Sharon Kendrick!*

BEHIND THE SCENES OF
SICILY'S CORRETTI DYNASTY

It's such a huge world to create—an entire Sicilian dynasty. Did you discuss parts of it with the other writers?

My story (which features an unbelievably sexy sheikh!) takes place mainly in Paris and the South of France, so my hero and heroine don't spend much time in Sicily. However, before my story starts, Rosa (my heroine) has a row with Lia (Lynn Raye Harris's heroine) and we discussed exactly what was said during this altercation.

How does being part of the continuity differ from when you are writing your own stories?

It's pretty fabulous to have a plot handed to you on a golden platter!

What was the biggest challenge? And what did you most enjoy about it?

My biggest challenge was making my hero able to respect a woman who started out by behaving like a bit of a tramp!

As you wrote your hero and heroine was there anything about them that surprised you?

I was surprised at how dark Kulal became once he'd married Rosa—even though the marriage was never meant to be anything but temporary.

What was your favourite part of creating the world of Sicily's most famous dynasty?

I liked Rosa's battle for independence and Kulal's courage in facing up to his demons.

If you could have given your heroine one piece of advice before the opening pages of the book, what would it be?

He's nothing but trouble!

What was your hero's biggest secret?

I don't think I can tell you Kulal's big secret, because it might spoil your enjoyment of the book.

What does your hero love most about your heroine?

He loves her spirit and her self-belief (which grows out of adversity).

What does your heroine love most about your hero?

sighs How long have you got? He's powerful, successful and super-confident, plus he also has a (deserved) reputation as a ladies' man. But Rosa can see through all the layers to the complex man beneath and it is that man she falls in love with.

Which of the Correttis would you most like to meet and why?

I'd like to meet all of Rosa's immediate and extended family because something tells me that it would be one hell of a party!

Available September 17, 2013

#3177 THE GREEK'S MARRIAGE BARGAIN
Sharon Kendrick

Lexi needs her estranged husband's help...even if that means playing the good Greek wife a little bit longer. The island sun can't match the reignited heat between them, but passion can't erase the memory of what tore them apart....

#3178 A FACADE TO SHATTER
Sicily's Corretti Dynasty
Lynn Raye Harris

Lia Corretti recognizes the shadows in Zach Scott's eyes. But there's nothing familiar about the hot heat of Zach as he traps her to him. Can she lower her guard long enough to let him see all of her?

#3179 THE PLAYBOY OF PUERTO BANÚS
Carol Marinelli

Innocent Estelle struggles to retain her cool at a society wedding when the most powerful man in the room makes her an outrageous offer: the money to settle family problems in exchange for a few months as Mrs. Sanchez!

#3180 NEVER UNDERESTIMATE A CAFFARELLI
Those Scandalous Caffarellis
Melanie Milburne

Raoul Caffarelli lived life in the fast lane until an accident confined him to a wheelchair and the care of Lily Archer—a beautiful woman unfazed by Raoul's arrogance. But both Lily and Raoul underestimate the power of the shared passion between them....

#3181 AN ENTICING DEBT TO PAY
At His Service
Annie West

When Jonas Deveson blackmails Ravenna Ruggiero into working as a housekeeper to pay off her debts to him, living under the same roof leads to unexpected and forbidden temptation, and Jonas is no longer sure who is being punished!

#3182 MARRIAGE MADE OF SECRETS
Maya Blake

Returning to their luxurious Lake Como palazzo after an earthquake, Cesare and Ava di Goia are strangers under the same roof. The bond between them is undeniable, but can the broken promises and secrets that drove them apart be overcome?

#3183 THE DIVORCE PARTY
Jennifer Hayward

Lily De Campo shows up to her lavish divorce party with one goal...leave minus a husband! But she is enticed back into Riccardo's glittering, gossip-fueled world where old insecurities resurface, and the media's golden couple must finally confront the truth behind the headlines.

#3184 A HINT OF SCANDAL
The Sensational Stanton Sisters
Tara Pammi

Olivia Stanton's name has been synonymous with scandal—every bad choice scrutinized in the headlines—but she's finally getting herself together. That is, until her twin disappears right before her wedding and Olivia's needed to stand in—as the bride!

YOU CAN FIND MORE INFORMATION ON UPCOMING HARLEQUIN® TITLES,
FREE EXCERPTS AND MORE AT WWW.HARLEQUIN.COM.

HPCNM0913RB

REQUEST YOUR
FREE BOOKS!

2 FREE NOVELS PLUS
2 FREE GIFTS!

PASSION
GUARANTEED
SEDUCTION

YES! Please send me 2 FREE Harlequin Presents® novels and my 2 FREE gifts (gifts are worth about $10). After receiving them, if I don't wish to receive any more books, I can return the shipping statement marked "cancel." If I don't cancel, I will receive 6 brand-new novels every month and be billed just $4.30 per book in the U.S. or $4.99 per book in Canada. That's a saving of at least 14% off the cover price! It's quite a bargain! Shipping and handling is just 50¢ per book in the U.S. and 75¢ per book in Canada.* I understand that accepting the 2 free books and gifts places me under no obligation to buy anything. I can always return a shipment and cancel at any time. Even if I never buy another book, the two free books and gifts are mine to keep forever.

106/306 HDN FVRK

Name _____ (PLEASE PRINT) _____

Address _____ Apt. # _____

City _____ State/Prov. _____ Zip/Postal Code _____

Signature (if under 18, a parent or guardian must sign)

Mail to the **Harlequin® Reader Service:**
IN U.S.A.: P.O. Box 1867, Buffalo, NY 14240-1867
IN CANADA: P.O. Box 609, Fort Erie, Ontario L2A 5X3

**Are you a current subscriber to Harlequin Presents books
and want to receive the larger-print edition?
Call 1-800-873-8635 or visit www.ReaderService.com.**

* Terms and prices subject to change without notice. Prices do not include applicable taxes. Sales tax applicable in N.Y. Canadian residents will be charged applicable taxes. Offer not valid in Quebec. This offer is limited to one order per household. Not valid for current subscribers to Harlequin Presents books. All orders subject to credit approval. Credit or debit balances in a customer's account(s) may be offset by any other outstanding balance owed by or to the customer. Please allow 4 to 6 weeks for delivery. Offer available while quantities last.

Your Privacy—The Harlequin® Reader Service is committed to protecting your privacy. Our Privacy Policy is available online at www.ReaderService.com or upon request from the Harlequin Reader Service.

We make a portion of our mailing list available to reputable third parties that offer products we believe may interest you. If you prefer that we not exchange your name with third parties, or if you wish to clarify or modify your communication preferences, please visit us at www.ReaderService.com/consumerchoice or write to us at Harlequin Reader Service Preference Service, P.O. Box 9062, Buffalo, NY 14269. Include your complete name and address.

HPI3

Nothing about this woman was typical. She wasn't afraid
of him, she didn't seem to want to impress him, and she'd
jumped, fully clothed, into a pool because she hated her
dress. And now she sat there glaring at him because he was
trying to be a gentleman—for once in his life—and make
sure she got back to her room safely.

She crossed her arms beneath her breasts and he fought the
urge to go to her, to tunnel his fingers into the thick mass of
her auburn hair and lift her mouth to his.

That was what she needed, dammit—a hot, thorough,
commanding kiss.

Hell, she needed more than that, but he wasn't going to do
any of it. No matter that she seemed to want him to.

And why not?

Tonight, he was a man who'd dragged a drowning woman
from a pool, a man who hadn't had sex in so long he'd nearly
forgotten what it was like. He wasn't a senator's son or an

All-American hero. He wasn't a broken and battered war vet. He was just a man who was interested in a woman for the first time in a long time.

More than interested. His body had been hard from the moment he'd stripped her out of that sodden pink dress, her creamy golden skin and dusky pink nipples firing his blood. He'd tried not to look, tried to view the task with ruthless efficiency, but her body was so lush and beautiful that it would take a man made of stone not to react.

Holy hell.

She stared at him defiantly, her chin lifting, and he had an overwhelming urge to master her. To push her back on the bed, peel open that robe and take what he wanted. Would she be as hot as those smoldering eyes seemed to say she would? Would she burn him to a crisp if he dared to give in to this urgent need?

"If you stay, you might get more than you bargained for," he growled.